An Artery

Kiana Firouz

Acknowledgements

In January 2021, I was recuperating from surgery in my Hastings flat during the pandemic lockdown. I couldn't leave my place and watched those walking tour videos on YouTube for a change of scenery. I contacted Stacey Williams, an amazing writer and wonderful person, to see if she was up for collaborating on writing a story for a movie about two womxns in their mid-40s on the road from London to Margate. We started exchanging emails, including music, pictures, and ideas. Finally, in early March, we had six pages of a beat-sheet of events for the story. Then lockdowns lifted, the weather was nice, approaching the summer, and we had to return to our day jobs. We let this project rest without discussion, as if we knew life had another plan. Little did I know that I would spend the next summer in Dubai to work on this story as a book. I even met Evelyn, and they touched on the final English draft. My Farsi is much better than my English.

England has always been kind to me. This endeavour has been a labour of love and appreciation. This story belongs to England. It's mine. It's Evelyn's, and it's Stacey's. And it's yours if you take this journey with us - a lovelike road trip.

Xx Kiana

CHAPTER *ONE*

London

The distant sound of a tap left rushing is the first thing that Beth heard when she stepped into the apartment, she expelled a soft swear under her breath; dropping the bags of grocery she'd been gripping and quickly rushing in the sound's direction. She reckoned it was coming from their shared bathroom. Carrie often forgot to turn off the tap after she was done using it; the first time she'd done it, Beth had found the action adorable and baffling—how did someone use something and walk away while using said thing? More than a year later, the action was less endearing and more exasperating. But then again, that was Carrie, absolutely uncaring when she wanted to be.

She walked into their bedroom; expecting to find Carrie sitting on the edge of the bed and tapping away on her phone, but the room was empty. Two loads of clean laundry were piled on each other on the bed but no Carrie. Beth headed into the adjoining bathroom and turned off the tap; crisis averted.

Now, to find Carrie.

"Carrie!" Beth called out, her voice echoing in the vacuum of their shared bedroom. Beth tried to shake off the chill that filled her; she didn't quite like the lifelessness of their apartment.

It was a riverside flat in London; merely a five minute walk from the River Thames. The entire neighbourhood was similar modern flats owned by wannabe tech people trying to create the British style social media platform and middle-aged people working from home. Carrie and Beth fell into the latter category; Carrie didn't have a job and Beth didn't need to work.

Most of the flats came furnished by interior design companies and always looked like something out of a magazine spread; the colour scheme was grey and white. It didn't feel like a home to Beth and she'd brought up the subject of redecorating every time but Carrie hadn't seemed interested in any of the occasions.

Beth called out Carrie's name again, louder; she was in the motion of shouting it again when she realised something. It was a little past eleven am and Carrie liked to do her Yoga in the hothouse. It didn't matter how many times that Beth had not so subtly hinted at the delicacy of the plants in the hothouse, Carrie did what Carrie wanted.

Two minutes later, Beth found Carrie; yoga mat and all, stretched dangerously close to a row of Venus Flytrap while generic pop music blared from her Bluetooth speaker— they were even the tamest plants in the hothouse and were displayed in tall glass showcases, compared to the other carnivorous plants that the hothouse housed.

Beth moved around the vast space, checking in on her babies, as she liked to refer to them in her head. The hothouse ran on a complicated system because of the plants in it; the lighting had to be on a specific level; the temperature and humidifiers needed to be regulated to make sure that they were also on the right level. She'd been told on several occasions by Carrie that her plants were just too high maintenance and at one point; irrational. That one had stung badly.

Still, Beth had put too much into this carnivorous plants business, not more than once she'd been accused of relying too much on her family's wealth and the stability of it. She'd wanted to prove everybody wrong and start a business of her own. She continued to make her rounds and just as she rounded the corner, she found a thermos flask on one of the shorter glass showcases which housed the Nepenthes-edwardsiana. It was Carrie's and she had the terrible habit of leaving her stuff around the greenhouse, in places that it shouldn't be.

Carrie's thermos flask sat on the glass showcase of a Venus flytrap. The flask rattled for a second before stopping. Inside of the showcase, the flytrap was curled in on itself; on a closer look, the plant had lost its sheen, a drying husk of what it used to be. The trap closed slowly, for the last time. It hadn't died due to a lack of attention; Beth had overfed it; choking it on affection until it could take no more.

Beth moved to stand in front of Carrie and cleared her throat. With great effort, Carrie untangled herself from the complicated position that she'd twisted herself into and paused her music. She was sweaty; blonde hair packed in a high ponytail, more than a few messy strands of hair had escaped from the ponytail and stuck to the sides of her face. Only Carrie could manage to look stunning even while doing exercise, to Beth it was like watching one of those sportswear commercials and seeing the models sweat elegantly, it didn't seem like something that happened in real life but here was Carrie, looking her best after a vigorous exercise. She had her hands on her hips and her lips twisted down in a small frown.

"What's the matter, Beth?" Carrie asked, there was the slightest bit of concern in her world as if the only reason she could phantom Beth interrupting her workout session had to be a serious emergency. There was no welcome greeting for her, even though Beth had informed her an hour ago when she left the house to go for a walk.

Beth waved the thermos flask like a red flag, "You left this on the showcase." She said, her voice sounding meek. This was how it was like whenever she tried to confront Carrie, she usually sounded apologetic instead of firm. The truth was that Beth found it hard to stay mad at Carrie for long; exasperated yes, but never angry.

Carrie blinked her long lashes as if she didn't quite understand what Beth was talking about. "And?" Her voice came sharply irritated now that she knew there wasn't some emergency.

Beth deflated, feeling all the fight leave her. "I've said it several times, Carrie, the hothouse runs on a tricky system and these plants survive under that."

Carrie blinked slowly, shook her head in exasperation, the end of her ponytail whipping left to right, "Beth, I understand that. What does that even have to do with anything?" Her voice was raised in the slightest, crossing the line from irritated to angry.

Beth couldn't help it, she flinched. "Well, I'm sorry. The plants are delicate things and the slightest change could upset their routine and they won't grow so well anymore. I've put a lot into this place, and I know you think otherwise but this isn't some dumb hobby, it's a business." Beth ranted, unable to stop the nonsensical flow of words.

She inhaled, trying to sound more rational and calm, "You can't just keep leaving things lying around here without picking them up." She thought of mentioning the tap that Carrie had left running as an additional example of her carelessness but she thought against it, she wanted to gently correct Carrie, not outrightly antagonise her.

Carrie flinched at her words, her eyes grew flinty and she blinked heavily as if she was trying to force back tears. Beth's heart sank all the way down to her stomach; she opened her mouth and tried to apologise but Carrie beat her to it.

"Well, I'm sorry to be inconveniencing your home, Beth." She spat out.

"Darling, I didn't mean that." Beth hurriedly added but she was ignored. Once Carrie got into the 'zone', nothing could get her out of it. Beth tried to ignore the pool of guilt swimming in her stomach.

She'd taken things too far this time; unlike Beth who had grown up privileged, Carrie hadn't had the same opportunity. She'd grown up the daughter of two stoners who cared more about getting high and thinking of the world as one big rainbow than they cared about their daughter. Carrie had once told Beth that her parents had never been downright cruel; their worst crime was absenteeism, to the point where a tween Carrie had learnt to fend for herself and to feed herself. More than once, she'd ended up in the care system. As a result of her upbringing or rather, a lack of one, Carrie was rather insecure about Beth's financial stability. She felt as if she was at Beth's mercy when it came to finances and she never failed to voice this out.

Beth tried her best to make sure that Carrie never felt this way; she was even careful to tiptoe around any topic that might make Carrie uncomfortable. Once, she'd made the mistake of asking Carrie about her earnings but Carrie had blown a fuse and they hadn't spoken to each other for days.

"Nothing in this house is mine anyways, I've always been at your mercy." Carrie continued saying, she took a step forward and snatched the mug from Beth's grip violently. "I'll just take my poor ass and leave your fancy business." She spat.

This was usually when she moved to act two of her meltdown; the tears came, streaming down her makeup free face. There was something beautiful about the way that Carrie cried; she didn't make any weird faces, tears just leaked out of her eyes while she angrily wiped them away. This was usually where Beth felt even more terrible about herself.

"Babe, I didn't mean that. All that is mine is yours – it has always been that way for the two of us." Beth said, taking a hesitant step closer to Carrie. She tried to reach for her hand but she was swiftly batted away.

Beth was grateful that she hadn't mentioned anything about the running tap. That would have for sure made things worse.

"Don't bloody patronise me, Beth!" Carrie shouted. "I'm not a fucking teenager."

"I think we just need more space," Beth began hesitantly. This was something she'd been thinking about for a while now. "The apartment is way too small for us. That's why we clash so much." She offered a wobbly smile that Carrie didn't return.

"Maybe if you didn't stake your claim on more than seventy percent of this place, then we wouldn't have this problem." Carrie hissed, not at all pacified by Beth's mention of space.

"I'm sorry." Beth said softly.

Carrie narrowed her eyes but she didn't say anything more; as if she sensed that there was no use in beating down an already beat down Beth. There was no fun in that anymore. Besides, she had won, there was no reason for her to still push the matter.

"This place is becoming a little too cooped up for the two of us." It was a hilarious thing for Beth to say because when they'd first rented the apartment, the real estate agent had gone on about the brilliantness of the house and how perfect it was for a young couple like the two of them; no kids, no pets. Just the two of them, it had sounded like a wonderful idea then to Beth too, in fact, she'd thought of the apartment along the lines of it being her dream home; a cosy enough place to live with her beautiful girlfriend.

"There's the place in Margate that my aunt left me in her will," Beth brought up hesitantly. The way Carrie blanched immediately would have been comical had Beth not been absolutely serious.

"You can't be serious," Carrie echoed. She shook her head from side to side as if trying to convince herself.

Aunt Bertha passed from a year long battle with cancer; she'd been Beth's favourite aunt, a womxn of her word who had a business mind unlike anybody else that Beth had ever known. She'd owned quite a few properties that had been shared to several family members. Beth had ended up inheriting a suburban home in Margate. The place already had sitting tenants and Beth had never quite thought of moving there until recently, maybe the stress of London was getting to them. Since she'd inherited the house, she'd begun to think that a change of scenery might be good for them.

"What would we even do in Margate?" Carrie asked with some contempt. Beth couldn't help but flinch at the vehement tone of her voice.

"There's plenty of things we could do. Our jobs are flexible – you work as an artist and I have a garden and extra space for plants to grow the business. We could commute to London whenever we need to, Margate is on the train line, and it's only a couple of hours away." Beth said and when Carrie was silent a beat too long, she added, "It would be a nice change of scenery, plus the house is bigger with about four rooms. You can even get the study converted to an art studio."

"I don't think that's a good idea, Beth," Carrie finally said. Her tone was final, bold for no reconsiderations. "Besides, what would we do with all that space, we don't even have a pet."

Beth bit her lip to keep from retorting. It was because of Carrie that they had no pets together. How many times had Beth approached the topic of getting a dog or even cats? Carrie had claimed to be allergic to the latter and to the former; she claimed that she wasn't ready for that kind of commitment. It had been heard for Beth not to take that one to heart. Had Carrie been unwilling to commit to a dog or to her?

"We could get a dog," Beth suggested, she wasn't surprised when Carrie immediately shook her head to the suggestion.

"What about the tenants?" She shot back. "You said the property in Margate already has sitting tenants."

Beth sighed, knowing to tread carefully because Carrie considered herself anti-capitalism. She hadn't failed to let Beth know on many instances that landlords were despicable people. "A friend referred to a law firm that specialises in property, I'm not saying that we move immediately. But we could consider our options, see if there is a way to settle with the current tenants and then we move in." That seemed like a perfectly sensible option to Beth but Carrie scoffed loudly, a sound that was full of derision.

"Spoken like a true capitalist." Carrie said.

Even though Beth had been called worse, she still flinched at the bite in Carrie's tone.

"This really isn't about capitalism." Beth began but Carrie was already speaking, working herself into a small pace, hands spread out as if she was giving a ted talk and not just talking to her girlfriend.

"It really is, Beth. The state allowing for private ownership of important resources has never and will never be a good thing. Land is a resource, Beth." Carrie said as if Beth already didn't know it. "One that is far too important to allow for private ownership and control of it. You've already made the decision to abuse the use of that resource by considering the options to evict innocent, working class people from homes they have paid for."

There was no use trying to get through to Carrie when she got into spiels like this one but Beth tried anyways.

"It's just an option to consider, babe, there would be no evicting innocent people. They would be compensated." Beth tried to get in.

Carrie whirled around, eyes sparkling with life; there was no sign of the previous crying womxn. "What if they've got kids, Beth?"

Beth grimaced, knowing well what was coming next and knowing that there was no way she could stop it.

"I told you of my own upbringing, Beth, of how my parents and I were booted out several times by cruel landlords. How could you want to do the same to other people?"

It didn't seem wise to point out that Carrie's parents had been evicted several times without number because they failed to pay rent when it was due.

"You're going to just chuck out a family with kids out into the streets?" Carrie repeated.

Beth just sighed, knowing that the battle was already lost. She tried to reason with the defeat; wasn't she out to make sure that Carrie was happy? If she claimed that she was happy right here in the city, in their Spartan looking home, who was Beth to deprive her of that?

***

Margate

"Jane, get off the counter."

The cat gave a sleepy meow but only settled further into the kitchen sink. The kitty had the habit of wandering into the sink to nap in, it didn't matter that it had a comfy space to sleep. The sink was her preferred choice.

Nancy sighed, a sound that was affectionate. Jane Doe as they'd named the cat wasn't actually owned by any of them living in the house, it had simply wandered in one day through the sliding doors that led to the back garden and kept coming back. Felicity began to leave a bowl of milk for it and so, the kitty continued to visit. Eventually, it became a regular in the house, staying past the evening time when it usually crept away outside the house.

Hunter hadn't liked it at first, thinking that the cat must belong to a neighbour and so they'd taken it to the local pet shelter to find out if Jane belonged to anybody.

They'd found out nothing from the shelter, and they waited for missing posters to turn up but hadn't. In the end, they'd claimed the kitty for themselves, a new member of the family.

Nancy dried off the last of the dishes and set them properly on the rack. She poured water from a jug into a clean glass and set onto a tray. She carried it and walked out of the kitchen and further into the house. She balanced the tray shakily on one hand and slid open the sliding door with the other hand.

Felicity was in the middle of the garden, half bent and tending to the cherry tomatoes that were as small as her thumb. She wore a straw hat that matched the pink of her sundress. Nancy stood for a moment, just watching her work. At last, Felicity rose to her full height and spotted Nancy. She waved vaguely at Nancy's protruding stomach.

Nancy smiled and placed the tray on the single table in the middle of the garden. Hunter planned to build a gazebo right in the middle of the garden. In the meantime, she sat on one of the chairs and sipped from the water, content with watching Felicity work. It would be her turn to tend to the garden tomorrow and then after her, it was Hunter's turn. For now, she let her bare feet sink into the hot afternoon sand.

Meanwhile, in the living room, an elderly womxn observed a younger man lying on the sofa – his name was Simon and he was Felicity's husband. He was pale and reedy thin. He shook slightly, a little uncomfortable under her piercing blue gaze. Her warm hands touched his cool, sweaty forehead, pushing back strands of hair framing his face and he flinched slightly.

"How are you feeling, Simon?"

He muttered something about feeling weak. She hummed a little and her hand left his forehead, she tilted his head to the side and two fingers went to his neck, feeling for his carotid pulse. She felt for what felt like an eternity; a stopwatch on the other hand.

Simon counted in his head, his mind straying to a hundred different scenarios, he closed his eyes, colour bursting behind his eyelids. When her fingers finally left his neck, he let out a tiny sigh of relief. He was free to finally lose himself in the dreamscape.

***

Carrie was still going on about the dangers of property owning and how she would feel terrible if a whole family and their four kids were cast out on the streets. Beth was growing increasingly irritated, she wanted to respect Carrie's decision to stick to London but she had the sinking feeling that all of Carrie's rants were excuses. She'd rather Carrie be forthright with the truth.

"And I don't believe in property ownership, Beth." She finished.

Beth inhaled, trying to keep her anger in check, knowing that Carrie would say that she was overreacting. "This is about trying to build our relationship, babe, nothing about communism or capitalism. Let's look into joint ownership options. We can speak to the property lawyers to look into our options." She dared to take a step closer to Carrie and hold her hands between hers. "I just love you and want to be with you in a place that is convenient for the both of us."

The truth was that Beth was afraid of Carrie leaving her; she'd been distant for a few months now, she was easily the chatty one in their relationship but she'd slowly become withdrawn, she stuck to her usual routine and never even tried to include Beth anymore. Beth was afraid that she was slipping away slowly, she was grateful for their rows at least, she'd read somewhere that having rows was healthy for a relationship. Couples had to fight and they ended up making up. All Beth just needed to do was make up with Carrie and she was willing to do whatever it took to keep her by her side.

Beth took Carrie's silence for contemplation and softened her voice even more, "Please, Car, let's just see the solicitors in a few days. Together, that's all I'm asking from you."

Beth didn't dare breathe until Carrie gave a little nod of her head. Beth took the liberty to pull her into a hug. She wasn't going to lose Carrie just like that, not when they had come this far.

Beth was sensitive, sweet and maybe even a little naïve in the sense that she was like a baby bird, seeking reassurance before flying or in her case, before making any decisions. Carrie found the trait endearing that she was such a pushover; it meant that she always got what she wanted. She didn't like that Beth seemed to be growing a backbone.

Still, Carrie couldn't help but smile a little, sipping leftover green smoothie in her glass. She sure had gotten her ways a lot of time arguing with Beth but she'd never been gifted joint ownership of a house. She had no intentions of moving all the way to fucking Margate, but if she played all the cards right, she could end up a homeowner. For all her spiel about being anti-capitalism and all that, it would be nice, very nice indeed.

CHAPTER *TWO*

Henry slammed a fist on the table as he roared with laughter, causing the water bottle standing upright on Anna's table to rattle a little. She frowned and held out a hand to stop it from falling. She didn't understand what was so funny in what Henry had said but the whole table was laughing – Gina had almost choked on a bite of her sandwich.

Anna was the only one sitting at the table with a small frown turning down her plump lips; she wiped the look of bafflement clean off her face before forcing a small chuckle that sounded more like a cough and stabbing her salad insistently with her fork. The sound came too late too, just when the laughter had died down. Her colleagues glanced at her with equal looks of puzzlement but they didn't say anything, didn't call her out on her usual quietness at lunch time.

To be honest, the last thing Anna wanted to do was to sit with these people; sure, they were nice enough people. She'd only been at the firm for five months but she'd quickly learnt that the solicitors at the firm liked to pretend as if they were one big family. Every last Friday of the month was company bonding time; usually in the form of group picnics or one activity or the other. Anna usually preferred her own company but in a firm like this one, she stuck out like a sore thumb for being introverted. So when Gina started inviting her to have lunch with some of the others, she didn't turn down the invitation. Every lunch time, she ate her food and let the chat become background noise. They'd all tried to include her but her monotone, one-worded answers soon stopped the barricade of questions.

Anna partly feared that Gina would stop popping into her office and asking her to lunch but her fear of ending up saying the wrong thing while talking trumped the fear of being kicked out of the group.

At her old firm, her bosses had referred to her as an efficient machine when it came to carrying out duties. They'd written her a good recommendation and her final pay-cheque had come with a big bonus.

Anna had tried her whole life to be liked but there was something about her, she either ended up saying the wrong thing to wrong person, and offending someone. So she'd rather stop trying.

"So I said, if it was me, I would of totally tapped that." Henry continued, his voice strained with barely constrained laughter. Anna had well zoned out of whatever story he was telling but her mind immediately zeroed in on his words.

"It would have." She cut in.

The table fell silent. Henry stopped mid chewing his burger.

"You said 'would of'" Anna made quotation marks in the air with her fingers. She didn't understand the looks she was getting. "Would Have." She paused, waiting for Henry to thank her. Then she realised that she'd done it again; corrected someone's grammar during a conversation. She winced at her mistake.

The whole table was still staring at her, this time with irritation rather than confusion. Gina refused to meet Anna's gaze when she tried to catch her eye.

'Well, thank you, Anna." Henry said sarcastically.

"Did you see what Dean did yesterday at the meeting?" Patrick cut in with the smoothness of someone who was an expert in the art of cutting through tension; a tact that Anna lacked. He sent her a small smile that was a little patronising. Still, Anna was grateful as the conversation resumed around the table again. She continued to stab at her salad, suddenly not hungry anymore.

Well, there was no expecting any invites from Gina to have lunch. Anna had fucked things up for good this time.

A few minutes later, Henry and Gina stood up, muttering something about how they had to get back to work. Anna watched them go, not even bothering to say goodbye. Patrick was still munching on an apple and Anna decided that she didn't want to be alone with him. There was no use pretending as if she was going to eat her salad anyways. She wasn't hungry anymore.

She stood up, her chair scraping back with a loud groan. She left her tray on the table – the cafeteria staff would pick it up – and headed towards the water cooler. She poured herself a cup and sips. She turned around and almost rammed into Patrick, she hadn't even known that he was standing behind her.

"Hey, Anna," He said with a smile, a tiny dimple popped from the corner of his chin. Anna found herself fixated on it. For some reason she didn't really like Patrick. He was too smiley, too friendly towards her. There were two types of people who reacted to Anna; the type of people who usually thought she was stuck up and rude. The second type of people was usually men who thought her closed off persona was a front and she was playing hard to get. Something told her that Patrick fell under the category of the latter.

She didn't want Patrick thinking that she was something that he could coerce out of its shell and fix like she was a broken doll. But she couldn't find it in herself to be rude to him either.

Her lips lifted up to the side in a robotic half smile.

"Patrick," She said.

"Hey, I just wanted to clear things up. Don't take things too seriously, it was just a joke." Patrick said with a lopsided grin.

Anna blinked, a little confused. She hadn't been taking anything too serious. She parted her lips to tell Patrick that but he was still speaking, gesticulating in a way that reminded Anna of a lawyer in court. Except, in their line of work, they didn't often go to court, at least not the kind in the movies.

"It's all just water cooler chat." Patrick added.

There was something about that particular sentence that pissed Anna off. Maybe it was because she was tired of being called too serious and stuck up.

Learn to take a joke, Anna, people usually say to her. Lighten up, it's not that serious.

She smiled a catty thing and flicked her eyes at the water cooler, the water bubbling slightly in the small tank. "What does that even mean? Water coolers don't make chitchat, they make for irritating background noise." She said snarkily, deliberating playing into the role of buzz kill.

Patrick gave her a puzzled smile, never one to be caught without a stupid grin on his face. He muttered the same excuse about returning back to work and left Anna standing there, right by the water cooler.

***

Carrie's hand moved leisurely down the bed sheet, slyly tugging the half cladding Tiff's upper body. She drew her lover in for a kiss, uncaring that the sheets slid down between them.

Tiff was like Carrie in so many ways; she was an artist for one and they'd met a year ago through a mutual friend's gallery opening and they'd started sleeping with each other a month later, just a few weeks shy of Carrie and Beth's three year anniversary of being together. Carrie enjoyed what she shared with Tiff, particularly because it was a no strings attached situation.

Tiff was carefree and confident in a way that Beth wasn't. Carrie did enjoy how she dominated Beth, how she looked at Carrie like a child waiting for guidance from her mother. Carrie enjoyed that but it got boring plenty of times. Tiff balanced the fun seeking side of Carrie. The most ironic part of it all was that Beth had met Tiff once but she thought she was merely another of Carrie's artist friends. Once a while, she would even ask after Tiff – because she was just that considerate.

Carrie usually passed on Beth's innocent greeting and Tiff would get a kick out of it. She thought that Beth was absolutely adorable.

Tiff was kissing her way down Carrie's neck when she gave a sudden giggle. Tiff paused.

"What?" A grin already spreading on her face. Carrie was thinking if she'd giggled in the middle of lovemaking with Beth, she would have thrown an insecure fit, her mind twisting into a hundred different possibilities of what she'd done wrong. But not Tiff, she was ready to laugh along to what Carrie was laughing about.

"It's Beth," Carrie forced out, her giggle turning into a fully throaty chuckle.

"What has Beth done again?" Tiff asked, leaning back against the headboard of the bed. Was it messed up that her other girlfriend knew so much about her main girlfriend? If it was, Carrie didn't really care.

"We got into another fight, can you believe Beth wants us to move to fucking Margate?" Carrie said, she still couldn't shake the incredulity in her voice. She didn't know what had gotten into Beth this time, what in the high heavens made her think that it would be a good idea to move their whole lives to a coastal town?

"Fucking Beth." Tiff said but she was laughing, even though she didn't yet know the punchline to the joke.

"She threw a fucking fit because of some dumb stuff I can't remember." Carrie continued, it was the truth, it had only been two days since they'd had that particular row but Carrie couldn't even recall what exactly had led to it. "And she started talking about some house in Margate that she inherited."

Tiff whistled, "Lucky bitch. I want to inherit a house too." There was real jealousy in her voice too. Tiff was a lot like Carrie except that she didn't have a wealthy girlfriend. She was the real definition of a struggling artist; she lived in a shabby apartment she rented with four others and barely avoided eviction each month. She wouldn't mind trading places with Beth for a day or two.

"So I told her there was no way I'm moving to Margate of all places – count me in when she inherits some villa in Spain or Sicily."

Tiff huffed a laugh at that.

"She went on and on about how moving would help our relationship and some other dumb stuff. Meanwhile, I'm giving a passionate speech on capitalism and shit." Carrie said, some of her old anger ignited at the remembrance of her row with Beth but the way Tiff snickered in the right places made her feel a little pacified.

"But she wasn't backing down at all, and she ended up offering joint ownership of the house." Carrie added, more than a little proud.

"No way." Tiff echoed.

Carrie's answer was a knowing smirk.

Tiff shook her head as if she couldn't quite believe it. "You better not be fucking kidding me, Car."

"I'm as serious as a heart attack, baby." Carrie answered; she couldn't deny that she liked the idea of owning property. Even though she might pretend otherwise to Beth. Carrie didn't like to remember her past, they were memories better left untouched. Her parents were one of those people who shouldn't have had a child because they hadn't the slightest idea how to raise one. Carrie had basically raised herself. She'd grown up learning how to cook basic meals so she didn't have to eat cereal all the time, she'd grown up left to the house for days on end – her parents forgetting that they had a daughter.

Carrie would do anything to never have to return to that absolute filth and poverty again. Even if it meant tricking poor, innocent Beth.

"My girl is a house owner," Tiff shouted. She raised a hand for Carrie to high five.

The two of them burst into giggles.

CHAPTER *THREE*

Anna opened one of the drawers in her desk, searching as if some hidden work she hadn't already completed would appear out of nowhere for her to do. She recalled her old bosses' comment about her being an efficient machine. If she was being honest with herself, they'd been right. She was efficient with her work; no use dallying about when she could do the work she was assigned to. She was meeting with some clients tomorrow to finalise the paperwork on their new property. All they needed to do was sign the papers and that was it.

She was reminded more than ever of how lonely she was. She tried not to think about it.

Anna restarted her laptop as she briefly mulled out going out tonight, the firm was already closing up for the day, she could head straight to a bar… and do what? Drink by herself? That would be too pathetic. She sighed as she loaded a game on her computer, might as well kill time as she waited in the office. The firm was open until 11pm and it was just 7pm; there was still plenty of time to kill. Maybe she should order takeaway.

She was still mulling over her options, distantly registering the voices outside her office, she heard Gina's laugh and thought she might have heard someone say her name but she was unsure.

The door creaked open and Patrick entered the office. Anna shared the space with him and another coworker but he was rarely in, in fact, his part of the office was bare; his table devoid of a computer, notes and any other memorabilia. She knew for a fact that he spent his time in Henry's office. The two of them were often working the same cases together so where he spent his time wasn't shocking at all. It was however shocking the rare times that he returned to his office.

"Hey, Anna, what's up?" He greeted, wearing his usual easy smile on his face. It didn't matter that Anna had been borderline rude to him earlier. Patrick was an easy going guy, too easy going. Anna wished that he would leave her alone and stop trying to be nice. "Hello, Patrick." She replied coolly.

He rubbed his palms together, the only sign of his nervousness. He'd discarded the jacket of his suit – probably in Henry's office – and his shirt was half out and the other half tucked in. He looked more like a prep school boy playing hooky rather than the hotshot lawyer he was trying to look like.

"So, a few of us headed out to the pub for beer and chips. There's also a game tonight, are you in?" He asked, still wearing that stupid smile of his.

Anna stared up at him with narrowed eyes. It didn't escape her notice that he was the one inviting her now. Prior to today's debacle at lunch, it would have been Gina seeking her out and begging her to let loose for one night. Frankly, Anna still didn't understand why Gina had bothered with her in the first place, the two of them were nothing alike in looks and in character. Gina had swishy blonde hair so light that it was almost platinum, she was bubbly and friendly and too goddamn perky. But it seemed that even perky Gina had her limits, now, it was Patrick left trying to be nice.

She bet that the others didn't want her to come to the pub with them, she bet that Henry was still a little salty about her correcting his grammar. They probably thought she was a killjoy but Patrick would have stuck up for her; c'mon guys, she has no other friends in the firm, let's be nice to her. It was like secondary school all over again.

"Sorry, Patrick," Anna began, not at all sounding sorry. "But I'm busy with some work here. I might stay late into the night."

For a brief second, Patrick's smile wavered before returning. "Ah, that's alright. Perhaps next time you can join us." There wouldn't be a next time, that much was certain.

Anna kept her eyes on him until he left the office, softly closing the door behind him. Outside, she heard him mutter something to someone and then a few seconds later, there was silence letting Anna know that they were all gone. Good for them, she hoped that they had plenty of fun. Her eyes returned to her computer screen where solitaire was loaded on the screen, the bright green background of the game taunting her.

***

Beth stared at her phone screen, reading the last message she'd sent Carrie; please, call me. Where are you?

A message that had been delivered and read more than forty minutes ago, if this piece of technology was to be believed then Carrie had received her message, read it and chose to ignore it, despite knowing well that Beth would be worried. It was past ten pm already and while Carrie did stay out late sometimes – she always claimed to be having drinks with friends, meeting with gallery owners and the likes – she always did tell Beth where she was going and when she might be back. This was the first time that she hadn't.

Beth wasn't so much afraid she was cheating as she was that Carrie was drifting away from her. Now they barely did anything together and Beth couldn't recall the last time that the two of them had gone out on a date. Not from a lack of trying on her part, in fact it was starting to feel like Beth did all the trying, all the caring and all the loving. Perhaps, Carrie had decided that it was all the duty of one person in their relationship to give all the fucks.

Beth was almost resigned to the fate of their relationship; sometimes she would sit down and think it might be okay for it to come to an end. But then the memories of their three year relationship would flash through her mind and she would break out in cold sweat at the thought of ending it, at the thought of being alone and the thought of the past three years becoming a waste. Didn't Beth once think that Carrie was the one? She'd thought of proposing not more than one occasion.

Now, she wasn't sure what to think anymore.

She lay on her back on the bed and heaved a heavy sigh; she rolled over and reached for her phone on the other side of the bed – Carrie's side. She checked if Carrie had replied her message but there was no new notification on her iPhone. She thought of sending another text but she didn't find it in her to do so. She closed her eyes and tried to sleep but all she could imagine was all the thousand different places Carrie could be right now, in the middle of the night.

Beth didn't sleep a wink that night.

CHAPTER *FOUR*

The receptionist at the solicitor firm was a womxn in her late fifties by the look of it; she looked like somebody's granny in her pink button up cardigan and welcoming smile. Beth returned the smile, albeit it was more than a little strained. As if the older womxn could sense it, her smile wavered a little and Beth couldn't help but wonder what the womxn saw when she looked at her. Did she see a young womxn on the verge of losing her mind? Because that was how Beth felt this morning.

She hadn't slept at all and it must show in the visible bags underneath her eyes; she'd made a half-baked attempt at applying makeup but she gave up, there was no use pretending that all was fine and dandy. It was Carrie who had the flare of pretence, Carrie who didn't show up last night and had left all of Beth's texts unanswered.

"Good morning, I'm Elizabeth Granger, I have an appointment with a solicitor this morning by 9am." She offered to the receptionist, who on a closer look had a badge on her cardigan that read Norma.

"Welcome, dear," Norma greeted, her voice cheerful in a way that was almost false. As if she sensed Beth's distress and thought that an extra dose of cheer might mask it. Beth appreciated the effort but saccharine sweetness was the last thing she needed now.

"I'll just confirm your appointment on my computer." Norma continued, if she was surprised that Beth had shown up an hour and thirty minutes earlier than said meeting time, she didn't show it. Then again, receptionists always saw the most wrongdoing in any organisation, they were very good at pretending otherwise.

Beth held tight to the long strap of her bag as if it may slip and fall off her shoulder if she didn't hold on to it properly. If only she could hold on to Carrie the same way.

"Alright, I've confirmed your appointment with Ms. Fenwick who is the solicitor that you made an appointment with. You may have a seat while you wait for her." Norma said, still smiling. Beth nodded.

"Is there anything I could get you? Maybe tea or a coffee?" Norma called out as Beth took a seat on one of the stylish metal chairs. The back of it was cool against her spine. Beth thought that it would definitely be impolite to ask for a stiff drink so she shook her head.

"A water is fine, thank you Norma." She said, lifting her lips up in a small smile. A few minutes later, she was nursing a bottle of water but there was still no Carrie. She jerked her right leg at a frenetic speed as she glanced at her phone. There was still no reply from Carrie.

She thought of facing the solicitor alone and was mortified at the thought; once again she was the only one putting effort into their relationship.

Beth ground her jaw together, feeling anger burn in her chest. Her fingers flew over the screen, typing another message.

Did you forget we have a meeting with the solicitor this morning?

She waited a beat, watched the blue check appear, indicating that her message had indeed been read.

Omw.

That was all she got from Carrie, not even the full sentence or an apology to follow. Well, at least she would be showing up. Beth let her shoulders relax a little. Ten minutes later, Carrie walked in through the revolving door, looking like she'd had the roughest night; her hair was dishevelled in a way that made Beth wonder if it was because she hadn't combed it or because someone had run their hands through it all night.

She was wearing the same clothes from yesterday; a lavender lace up ruffle blouse that was now ruffled in more ways than one and there was a small red stain on the right sleeve. She was wearing sunglasses that matched the brown of her palazzo pants. She didn't immediately spot Beth and went straight for Norma. Beth caught Norma's slight flinch as Carrie leaned in.

"Carrie," Beth snapped her lover's name. Two pairs of eyes turned to her. Dear Norma tried and failed to hide the curious light in her eyes, her gaze shifting from Beth's to Carrie's in a way that reminded Beth of a shark out for blood.

Carrie shot Beth a thin smile and turned to face Norma once more.

"Can you tell me where the bathroom is?" She asked Norma.

Norma wordlessly pointed at the hallway.

Beth dashed after Carrie, footsteps clicking loudly on the pristine white tile of the floor.

"Carrie!" Beth said, her voice almost a roar of outrage. She followed Carrie, but she was faster, practically dashing towards the restroom with one hand slapped over her mouth. Was she about to throw up?

Carrie got to the end of the hallway and went inside the last door on the right. She shut the door with a resounding bang. Beth didn't bother running after her again, she reduced her pace to a brisk walk and came to the restroom. She entered and found Carrie dry heaving in one of the stalls.

"This is absolutely ridiculous, Carrie." Beth said. "Absolute bollocks. This isn't just something that should be important to me alone, it's about our future. Where were you last night? Are you ill? "

She heard the toilet flush. Carrie stepped out, eyes blazing with fury. She was close enough to Beth that she could smell the alcohol on her clothes. Beth's nose scrunched up.

"You were out drinking." She didn't know why disappointment coloured her tone. Carrie going out to drink with friends and giving Beth no heads up that she wouldn't be returning home was totally a Carrie thing to do. It hurt Beth so much because in the early stages of their relationship, she recalled a totally different womxn, one that had been as committed as Beth was to their relationship. Now, this womxn standing before her, reeking of alcohol and lips tightened stubbornly Beth didn't recognize at all.

"I'm here, aren't I?" Carrie said, with an effusive eye roll. "There you go again, blowing things out of proportion. I'm here, aren't I? And I'm not even late." She glanced down at her wrist. It was bare and pale like her face. Beth was struck by how plain Carrie looked that morning; there were little bags under her eyes and her fair skin took one a sickly milky hue. "The meeting is for…" She trailed off, unable to recall their appointment time.

It struck Beth that Carrie must have gone to their apartment first, she must have gotten there and found out that Beth wasn't home, deducing that she must have headed to the solicitor alone. Had she even remembered that they were supposed to be seeing a lawyer today? Or had she realised at the last minute and dashed down here?

"Right, you don't even bloody remember, do you?" Beth shouted.

"Why does that even matter?" Carrie shouted back, jabbing a finger at Beth's chest. "I'm here, Beth, I'm fucking here. Why do you have to hold everything over my head like you're my parent? You always love to belittle me, make me feel inferior to you because you're oh so fucking special. So fucking entitled."

Beth flinched, but her anger didn't abate. She couldn't stand Carrie talking to her like that, throwing accusations as she usually did when Beth tried to stand up for herself. Not a single day had Beth felt like Carrie was inferior to her in any way and not certainly in the financial sense. Beth was sick of being reminded of her privilege every time. She knew that she was extremely lucky to be born into a rich family, to inherit money and properties and everything else. She was extremely grateful too and she didn't try to distort the truth with rose coloured glasses. She was very well aware that not everyone had a trust fund like she did; she'd never for once made Carrie feel like she was inferior – she paid every bill and never for once asked Carrie to pay her back or compensate in one way or the other.

Even when it came to the fucking grocery. She didn't understand where Carrie's insecurities stemmed from but she'd never made them seem irrational. So why did Carrie always insist on bringing them up?

"Where is this even coming from, Carrie? My goodness, I'm talking about you ghosting me yesterday and showing up hungover to an important meeting and I'm the bad guy here? How does that even work?" Beth threw her hands up in exasperation.

Carrie sidestepped her and walked to the sinks to rinse her hands. "Fine, you're right and I'm wrong. Happy?" She conceded with a scoff. Beth wasn't the least bit happy, mostly because their argument didn't feel like a victory won. She suspected that it didn't matter how many times she explained it to Carrie, she just would never understand. Beth didn't at all enjoy exchanging words with the womxn she loved. It didn't make her feel on top of the world either. She just wanted Carrie to see their relationship, to understand Beth's concern and to be concerned herself. It seemed like that was too much to ask for.

Carrie splashed water on her face and Beth wordlessly pulled out a handkerchief from her purse and handed it to her. She took it without a word of thanks and merely dabbed her face with it gently.

"Let's just get this over with." Carrie said dispassionately.

"Where were you last night?" Beth had to ask.

Once again, Carrie's defensive hackles immediately rose up. She met Beth's eyes in the mirror and heaved a sigh. "What does it matter now? I'm here, let's get whatever papers we need to sign."

Beth didn't correct her on that front. "You're here, Carrie. You're here stinking of booze and looking a damned mess. Where were you?"

Carrie didn't meet her eyes, "I was out with friends. What does it matter?"

Beth narrowed her eyes, there was something fidgety about Carrie that she didn't quite trust. Heck, Beth didn't even know if she could trust her anymore. Carrie mistook Beth's quietness for hesitation and continued to speak.

"Let's just go and sign this thing." She pressed.

Beth laughed harshly, the sound exploding in the echoing space. Carrie flinched and Beth couldn't help the thin smile that spread on her lips. "For someone who thinks owning property is theft, you sure are excited to be a homeowner." She couldn't help the jab either.

Although, she felt no satisfaction in the cold look that Carrie shot her. She was struck with the sudden urge to apologise, this might be the first time in a while that Beth was holding her own in one of their fights. She usually backtracked the moment that Carrie got furious, she usually let the peace reign – at least for one more day. That was her motto. She didn't like fighting Carrie but she couldn't deny that she felt a little better hashing out all of her bottled up grievances.

Until she realised that there was someone in the next stall, it was the distant sound of the toilet flushing that let her know and something told Beth that whoever was inside had deliberately done that, to let her know that they were in there. Somehow, it felt like a gesture of support; I see you and I hear you.

Meanwhile, Carrie was still ranting. "Maybe some of us get tired of fucking the landlady to cover for rent all the time."

There was a cough from the right stall and Carrie halted mid speech, she gave Beth a pointed look; only realising that someone was in the restroom with them.

Beth was still reeling from the shock of Carrie's last words and left speechless at how Carrie always belittled the dynamics of their relationship. She parted her lips to speak but no words came out. At the same time, the door to the other bathroom stall opened and out stepped a young womxn; maybe a year or two younger than Beth. Her face was passive – you would never guess that she'd heard most of Beth and Carrie's argument. She wore a brown suit and penciled skirt that hugged her lithe form. She passed Beth and Carrie. The latter didn't appear to notice her but Beth definitely caught the slight look of sympathy that was sent her way.

The womxn walked to one of the sinks and washed her hands. She lingered a little, taking longer lathering her hands with soap.

The awkwardness in the restroom was palpable. Carrie didn't seem to notice the exchange of looks that Beth had shared with this womxn though; she was assessing the womxn not so subtly with a hint of impatience. Beth wondered what Carrie thought of her but there was every chance that Carrie wasn't even actually looking at the womxn but rather, at her clothes. She was possibly measuring how much her shoes had cost. Growing up privileged herself, Beth had grown up being surrounded by designer things, she knew how to identify expensive clothes and this womxn had good taste. Carrie also had an eye for fashion, it was actually one of the few things that she had in common with Beth.

Finally, the womxn stopped washing her hands and stepped out of the restroom, with one final lingering glance sent Beth's way.

"Look, I'm sorry for showing up late. I didn't think that I would be staying out that late but a few old friends were in town and we were catching up. I didn't invite you because you didn't know them and you have this habit of getting awkward around new people. Things got a little out of control and I was too drunk to come home, so I stayed in a hotel instead." Carrie explained.

Beth blinked, a little surprised by the sudden rush of words from Carrie. Carrie didn't really apologise often, if this instance could even been deemed an apology – Beth hadn't missed the slight dig at her introverted persona. But it was as good as Beth was going to get. Besides, wasn't this whole deal about trying to be closer as a couple, to mend the rifts between them? It wasn't a too bad first step and for the first time, Beth didn't stop the surge of hope rising in her chest. She reached for Carrie's hand and gave it a light squeeze. They were back in the waiting room, ten minutes before the start of their appointment.

If this was a first, fresh start, Beth didn't mind taking it with Carrie.

"It's fine, I overreacted a little." Beth said. She wasn't sure she was telling the truth in that moment, maybe in a few days she might come to regret her outburst in the restroom a few minutes ago but right now? Beth didn't feel a single lick of regret. Hadn't that outburst set Carrie straight? She couldn't bring herself to be the slightest bit remorseful. Carrie leaned in, resting her head on Beth's shoulder and although Beth couldn't see her face, she could tell that Carrie was smiling and because of that, she too began to smile. If only she knew that Carrie was smiling for a totally different reason.

CHAPTER *FIVE*

Anna was more than a little surprised when Bathroom Stall Womxn and her girlfriend stepped into her office. She'd heard of how fate had a funny sense of humour but for the first time she was beginning to understand that saying a little.

The truth was, Anna had been in that stall to hide from Patrick. He seemed to have suddenly remembered that he had his own office space and he'd come in this morning and headed straight for her, to regale her with the juicy story of their outing at the pub last night, as if Anna cared – she didn't, not even a little bit. But boy did Patrick not know how to take a fucking hint.

He'd perched himself on the edge of her desk, uninvited and uncaring as he told the story of how apparently, Henry had gotten drunk and puked during karaoke. Anna hadn't been able to stand the small talk – really, one of these days, she would have to tell Patrick that it was okay that she didn't fit into his group and that he didn't have to keep treating her as if she was a charity case; the weird nerd with no friends at lunchtime. They weren't in high school anymore.

So she'd pretended that she needed to make an important phone call; she'd all but sprinted out of her office, leaving him no doubt gaping after her and possibly concluding that she was in fact more than a little insane. She knew that she had an early appointment with some new clients soon so she couldn't leave the building and just go for a walk. She hadn't wanted to be seen in the cafeteria either so she'd gone downstairs and hid in the guest restroom, checking email on her phone.

Anna had been seated in the cramped stall for almost ten minutes when she heard the door open and then chaos ensued. The first womxn 'Beth' had been furious at her girlfriend, complaining about her flakiness. Anna had been amused at the drama, at least that was until 'Carrie' opened her mouth to talk. Carrie was a real pain and unapologetic about it too. It had taken everything in Anna to remain in the stall and not come out to verbally defend Beth. Which was a weird feeling for Anna, most people she'd come to discover didn't quite understand her and in return, she'd found herself clumsy and distant from most people but with 'Beth', Anna had felt the unusual need to defend her, to show support in whatever way she could. Maybe because she'd listened to Beth trying to get her girlfriend to listen to her. Maybe that was what Anna had felt a kinship with; being misunderstood and left unheard countless of times.

Even though Anna couldn't have said a word – she didn't like to get involved in other people's drama – she'd still tried to let 'Beth' know that she had someone on her side. So she'd flushed the toilet like an idiot and then came out of the stall to give 'Beth' pointed looks that she didn't think the other womxn understood. She'd thought that was the end of it too, that leaving that restroom meant never seeing Beth or her girlfriend again. But fate was funny like that.

It turned out that Anna's new client was Beth and Carrie. The moment Beth stepped into the room and her eyes fell on Anna's, she recognized her. Anna could tell by the slight pause in her steps before she took the offered seat. Carrie on the other hand must truly live in her ass because she frowned at Anna with not a single ounce of recognition. What a prissy. She didn't understand how a womxn like Carrie came to be with a womxn like Beth. Anna had heard the story of how opposites attract too many times to count, she'd never been so sorry to see an example in the flesh.

"Good morning, I'm Anna Fenwick and I'm the solicitor you made an appointment with." Anna said with a perfect, robotic smile on her face, usually she tried to muster a little more than a stiff smile for her clients but she couldn't bring herself to be more civil than necessary to Carrie. Especially since she didn't seem to be paying any attention to Anna; her eyes were roaming Anna's office, taking in everything in the same way one would mentally catalogue the items in a clothing store. That look was purely calculating and Anna didn't like the look of it. She forced herself to focus on Beth who was smiling a little.

She was beautiful. The thought popped into Anna's head, unbridled. She was petite with a round face that looked friendly. Honestly, to Anna, she didn't look a day over twenty one. Her face was almost bare of any makeup, save for the dash of red lipstick on her shapely lips. Her eyes were a bright blue that were earnest, friendly – if a little tired. She wore a button up coat and sat straight, with one leg crossed over the other. There was a certain grace about her that was compelling. Anna shook her head, trying to free it of the thoughts that were forming. This womxn was her client, she shouldn't be thinking of her in such an uncouth manner.

"Nice to meet you, Miss Fenwick." Beth paused. "Is it Miss?"

A ghost of a smile flickered on Anna's lips. "Yes, I'm not married."

"Oh, I'm Elizabeth Granger, just call me Beth." She offered.

Anna briefly wondered if she too could ask Beth to call her by her first name. It was a perfectly harmless offer but Anna hesitated, it felt like crossing some unseen line. Anna didn't make a thing out of inappropriate relationships with her clients. Not more than one occasion, she'd heard some of them describe her as cold. She could do to be a little more friendly, one had said. But in the end, it hadn't mattered because she did her job efficiently. She pursed her lips in response to Beth's offer and thought she saw something like disappointment flash through Beth's blue eyes as if she'd expected Anna to extend the same offer. Anna felt her stomach clench, she hated the thought of disappointing Beth.

Something told her though that Beth was a people pleaser. It was likely the basis for her relationship with Carrie. She looked to Carrie for constant validation and was constantly taken advantage of too. The realisation angered Anna.

"This is Carrie Rupert, she's my partner." Beth continued smoothly, having caught on that Carrie probably wasn't going to make any attempt to introduce herself. Also used to covering for her uncouth girlfriend, Anna noted to herself.

Carrie however, flicked her hair to the side as if she was seated front row at a fashion show. Anna narrowed her eyes; she'd received the details about Beth's and Carrie's little situation and according to those files, Beth was the one who had recently inherited a house from her late aunt. She didn't understand why Carrie was acting like she was entitled to it, or as if because her girlfriend was well to do meant she too was automatically the same thing. Except, she was starting to look down on Anna, starting to see her as hired help to sort out the mess they were in.

Not only a terrible girlfriend but incredibly vapid, Anna noted mentally. She could have continued to observe Carrie's behaviour like a psychologist would regard an experiment but frankly, it was a waste of time and Beth was talking; Anna would rather pay attention to her and so she did.

"This firm comes highly recommended to me, a friend of mine has used the services of this firm. I hope you're able to help us with what is clearly a delicate situation for us." Beth said. Although she was smiling, Anna detected the undercurrent of nerves in her voice. She didn't really understand why this house was so important to Beth and Carrie but it clearly was.

Anna narrowed her eyes, a little lost in her thought. Her first guess was that Carrie was pressuring Beth, trying to get her to give her a part of the inherited house. She'd heard as much in the bathroom. She hoped that she was wrong, because the thought of Carrie – who was very clearly manipulative – tricking Beth into doing something that she didn't want to make Anna unsettled. She didn't want to meddle, in fact, she was pretty sure that she would be breaking some company rules if she did but if it was a case of manipulation, Anna really didn't think she could sit back, fold her hands and do nothing.

She blinked and realised that Beth's smile was frozen, she was clearly waiting for verbal reassurance from Anna. Carrie on the other hand just looked irritated as if she'd rather be somewhere else. She kept fidgeting on the edge of her seat, looking uncomfortable.

Anna paused, trying to regain control of their exchange. "I assure you that we'll look at the best options concerning your inheritance and the technicalities of it all. I've already gone through your file and have a few suggestions on how to go about the situation – it's all very cut and dry here."

Days ago when Anna had received the file on Beth's inherited house in Margate and her desire to share ownership with her girlfriend and move into the place, she'd thought that it would be a little difficult for that to happen; seeing as there were already tenants occupying the place. She also didn't understand why Beth wasn't content being landlady and collecting all that sweet rent money. She sensed that there was a personal reason in there somewhere.

She wondered if it was a topic that she could subtly bring up.

"There isn't anything to look into." Carrie cut into the conversation with a snotty tone of voice, she sounded as if she thought Anna was stupid for even daring to suggest otherwise. "We have decided to jointly own the place in Margate. Shouldn't you be drawing up the paperwork for that already, Miss Farwick?"

Anna ignored the very deliberate mistake of her name. She didn't plan on stooping down to Carrie's level of pettiness. She hadn't gone to law school for years to squabble with someone who didn't even know what they were talking about. She hadn't failed to notice how Carrie didn't want to discuss the very idea of moving into the house, it appeared to Anna that Carrie was just interested in owning the house.

Anna almost smiled too but refrained from doing so, she didn't want to give little petty an outright reason to be rude. Besides, even though Anna might hope it was otherwise, Carrie did have plenty of sway on Beth and wasn't afraid to use it. And it seemed that Carrie wasn't stupid; she knew that there would be a long legal process before she and Beth would be able to move into the house in Margate. The first step would be trying to settle with the tenants first and that was a negotiation that wasn't so straightforward and mightn't even work. The next step would be to go to court and that would be long, possibly messy and Carrie knew it. In fact, she was probably banking on it. All she was interested in was the promise of joint ownership. Anna didn't want to play right into her hands.

"Well, of course, all the paperwork has been drawn." Anna began slowly. Carrie didn't wait for her to finish.

"Excellent! Then we can sign right now, right babe?" She looked at Beth with a look of saccharine sweetness. It was clear as day to Anna that Carrie didn't love Beth.

Anna's eyes met Beth, calm. She tried to convey in that look that there was no pressure, that she was allowed to think rationally about what step to take next before making such a huge decision. Anna had handled a few cases like theirs, actually; bitter exes who wanted to find a way to kick their ex out of the joint ownership they'd shared on a property. It was always a messy process that didn't usually end well. She didn't want Beth to hate herself in the future.

Beth bit down on her lower lip and gave a single nod. "We would like to jointly own the house." She agreed with Carrie.

Carrie gave Anna a triumphant smirk. Anna just stared back with her usual cool.

"Well, that is certainly a huge step to take. How long have you two been together?" She injected some of that saccharine into her own voice.

Carrie's look of confidence wavered a little, clearly not understanding Anna's change of tone and more than a little wary of it. If only she would understand that Anna didn't care about sparring words with her. Anna was concerned about Beth, she wanted to make sure that she wasn't coerced into making any decisions that she would regret in the future. If Carrie happened to be humiliated in the process, Anna didn't mind.

"Three years." It was Beth who answered.

Anna smiled as if she cared.

"That's beautiful." She said; she might have meant it too if she hadn't witnessed the scene in the bathroom. Anna wasn't against relationships or the concept of love. She is doing just fine on her own but she was also a believer of facts and there were just too many examples of true love that she'd witnessed that she couldn't pretend as if it didn't exist.

"Yes." Carrie said with a smug look on her face. She thought she was out of the woods now.

"But, I must recommend that this is a decision that the two of you think through carefully. Sharing ownership of a house can be very messy. I've dealt with clients who regret the decision to share joint ownership of their houses with their partners and it's often a messy process to undo." Anna chose her words carefully, not wanting to offend Beth. Even though Beth seemed taken by Carrie and was likely willing to do anything she asked because she loved her, Anna still believed that she could get through to Beth, she might be in love but she wasn't stupid.

"I advise that you consider other options – or at the very least, see the house first before making any decisions."

Carrie scoffed, the derisive sound cutting through the silence. She smiled a bland smile. "Let me get this straight, Miss Freewick, you're trying to dissuade us from taking a very important step in our relationship because of what? You're concerned about our relationship in the instance that we break up? How messed up is that?"

"That is it with you lawyers, reducing humans to mere words on a contract." Carrie added almost bitterly. If Anna didn't know better, she might have thought that Carrie had a grudge against lawyers.

Anna noticed the way Beth immediately tensed up. So this was how Carrie usually won their arguments, by resorting to dramatics and playing the victim. Anna however wasn't the least bit affected by Carrie's dramatics, neither did she feel a need to placate her.

"I am in no way trying to prevent what is obviously an important milestone in your relationship." Anna clarified calmly. "Nor trying to dissuade you two from the process of joint ownership. As your solicitor, my job is to provide you with legal advice on your situation and that includes making sure that you're well informed about the decision that you're about to take."

Beth and Carrie shared a look. The former wore a sour look on her face, clearly knowing that she'd been outwitted and not liking it at all, if Anna was to go by the looks she was being shot at.

"I agree with you." Beth said a little too quickly. She didn't meet Carrie's indignant look.

This time, Anna did allow herself to smile a little. "Excellent, I'm glad that we're on the same page. I personally recommend the inclusion of a get out clause in the case of an unfortunate split."

It was a miracle that Carrie didn't lunge from her seat and reach out to claw out Anna's throat. She looked as white as a sheet though, something akin to fear flashing in her eyes.

"I agree with everything you've said," Beth repeated. "But Carrie and I have a trusting relationship, there will be no need for such a step." She added firmly. It took a slow second for her the implications of her words to dawn on Carrie but when they did, a wide grin stretched her face, lighting it up. Although Anna didn't want to accuse Beth of being shallow, she could start to see a little why Beth was enamoured with her in the first place. She was beautiful, in a dainty doll kind of way. A typical beauty queen. She shot Anna a triumphant look. "Where do we need to sign?" She asked coolly.

Somehow, Anna managed to keep a cool front even though she saw red. She was angry, she realised. Maybe a little at Beth for clearly seeing Carrie's tactics and not fighting back against it. But she was angrier at Carrie, for being so openly horrible.

Anna had been a lawyer for plenty of years enough to know how to deal with infuriating clients. She was not going to lose her cool and give in to the urge to clobber Carrie with the umbrella that she usually kept under her desk for when it rained. Anna flipped open the file in front of her and slid several papers towards Beth, deliberately ignoring Carrie. She'd drawn up the paperwork yesterday without giving much thought to it. Now, she wanted to rip it to shreds.

Beth wordlessly slid the papers to Carrie to sign first.

Carrie looked up with a saccharine smile pointed at Anna like a mocking weapon. "Can I get a pen?"

Anna handed her one.

She watched as Carrie signed on the pages, her signature flowery, bold, taking up more space than necessary and absolutely unnecessary – more than a little like she was. She slid the papers to Beth's side of the table and handed her the pen.

CHAPTER *SIX*

The afternoon sun streamed in through the windows. Everything in the room was white; from the sheets on the bed to the white curtains that had pushed to the ends to allow sunlight into the room. The man wearing black laying on the bed stood out like ink splashed on the sheets. He was fast asleep or at least looked to be that way. The older womxn; Susan observed him from where she sat stood at the foot of the bed; she glanced down at the watch on her wrist with a slight frown marring her face.

For the better part, her subject; Simon was unresponsive. Still and almost lifeless, one might think if it wasn't for the steady rising and falling of his chest as he breathed. Susan continued to watch the rise and fall of his chest, she'd already noted the steadiness of his breathing earlier; nothing seemed to be amiss.

A frown bloomed on her weathered face, that too was the problem – that nothing seemed to be happening. Her subject had been in this state for the past few days. Although it was too far early in her experiment to know for sure, but something ought to have been happening by now. She'd administered the proper doses, fixed up this room to create the perfect ambiance that would get him into the right state. Still, nothing.

Susan liked to think of herself as patient; one didn't get to her age without a great deal of perseverance and patience. But some of that patience was stretching thin.

She was about to call it a day and leave Simon alone when a small sound broke the careful, almost artificial silence in the room. Susan took a step forward and caught the small movement of his chapped lips as they parted and made that small sound again. Susan wasn't one to pump a fist in celebration but she almost did that.

Finally. Something was happening.

She glanced down at her watch to note the time and swiftly scribbled on the small notepad she'd cradled to her chest, her eyes not leaving the male form on the bed. She thought that might be the end of it but she leaned closer, catching the fluttering of his eyelids. At first, she feared that he might wake, the action was repeated but he didn't stir.

Susan continued to scribble, a smile forming in the corner of her lips. Things were starting to go according to her plan.

***

Beth stared down at the paper in front of her as if she didn't recognize it; Anna immediately placed the deer caught in the headlights stare. There was slight doubt on her face as if for the gravity of what she was about to do was sinking on her shoulders for the first time ever. Besides her, Carrie's smile grew rigid, she gave Beth a slight nudge to her side and smiling through gritted teeth.

"What are you waiting for, babe?" She asked with a shrill laugh. "Sign the papers, let's move on to the next phase of our lives."

Anna observed Beth for a candid moment; there was fright in her eyes that she tried to blink away when she noticed Anna's eyes on her. She looked up from the paper and cleared her throat, her left hand reached for the pen but before she could pick it up, Anna leaned forward and swiped both the document and paper right from her.

"What the fuck?" Carrie snapped. Beth looked shell shocked but there was something like relief in the way her shoulders relaxed a little.

Anna was careful to keep all kinds of emotions off her face. Carrie could accuse her of being emotionless and reducing her relationship into another statistic but it was better than being accused of being attached to Beth even though this was the first time Anna was meeting the both of them. She could imagine Carrie and Beth getting home, Carrie trying to spin the story.

"She fancies you! Did you see the way that she couldn't stop looking at you?" Carrie might say.

Beth would hesitate, disbelieving but wanting to pacify Carrie above every other thing. She would probably end up agreeing with Carrie and then her subsequent request for a different solicitor, maybe even a whole new firm. No, Anna couldn't afford to mess this up for Beth.

"I really advise that you see the house first." She began carefully, knowing that she needed to phrase her words in a way that was logical,

logical enough that Carrie couldn't weasel from it with theatrics. "As your solicitor, it is my job to make sure that you end up with the best possible case scenario to prevent any regrets in the future."

Carrie parted her lips to speak but Anna beat her to it.

"This has nothing to do with your relationship; I'm glad that that front is well secured." She continued. She didn't fail to notice how Beth sighed in relief at that one. For the first time, Anna realised that Beth was embarrassed that she'd witnessed their spat in the bathroom. She hoped that Beth didn't think she was being sarcastic with her assessment of her relationship with Carrie – well, Anna didn't exactly mean the words either but she wasn't being sarcastic.

"But there are other angles to cover, other points of view to look at this from. Is the property suitable for you? Will the tenants be willing to reach a settlement? And if they don't, would taking the legal route be a pointless and exhausting battle for the two of you?" Anna tried to infuse a little sympathy into her voice as she spoke, she'd never done this for any of her clients, never tried to be anything more than efficient and factual but here she was, breaking her rules for a womxn she just met.

It seemed to be working though; Beth was worrying her lip in consideration and even Carrie was silent. Anna got the sense that Carrie was desperately working out a way she could get out of this.

"You're right, Miss Fenwick." Beth finally admitted. "What would we do?"

Anna was sure there was a smug little smile playing on her lips as she said the next words. "I'll phone up the house now and set a meeting for today. We'll get there by car, it'll be a very quick trip back and forth."

Now Carrie was the one looking like a deer caught in the headlights. "Is that possible? Under such short notice." She gave a trifling laugh. Nobody joined in. She turned a little in her seat to face Beth, "Babe, you can't be seriously considering this trip? What will happen to the plants?"

A brief look of surprise flashed through Beth's eyes at the mention of plants, if Anna had to guess, she'd say that the plants was something Carrie had never shown much concern for in the past.

"I think we should listen to the lawyer, Car," She gave a little laugh of her own. "Besides, it's just Margate, a two hour drive tops from London to there."

Anna scrolled through the map on her phone. "An hour and thirty five minutes in normal traffic according to Google."

Carrie shot her a venomous look that she chose to ignore.

"See," Beth was still trying to pacify her. It was like trying to calm down a bratty toddler crying for sweets. Didn't it ever get exhausting for Beth. "Under two hours. It can be a nice road trip."

Carrie rolled her eyes, "it isn't a bloody road trip if our lawyer is coming with us."

Anna smiled blandly at that. That was kind of true. It seemed that Carrie finally got the memo that there would be no weaselling out of this one, her shoulders slumped in defeat and she sniffed pathetically, perhaps trying to see if she could summon the waterworks and get Beth to change her mind.

"Fine." She mumbled.

Anna looked up from her phone as if she hadn't been paying close attention to their conversation. "Excellent, I'll make the call." She made Beth confirm the phone number for the residence in Margate and dialled it.

The first two phone calls went unanswered and Anna caught Carrie trying so hard not to smile.

"Oh, well, maybe today's not just a good one for them. We can always try again another day."

Anna ignored her, she hadn't become a lawyer by quitting early. She dialled the residence for the third time and this time, someone answered.

"Hello, Parker's residence." A lilt female voice came. "Who's calling?"

"Good morning, I'm Anna Fenwick, a solicitor in London representing my client; Elizabeth Granger, who became the landlady for the property." Anna said briskly.

There was silence for a second before the voice came again, this time with none of the warmth in her voice; only wariness. "Anna Fenwick." The womxn echoed Anna's name.

"You may address me as Fenwick. My client and I are coming to have a look at the place today, just some protocol that should have been done when Ms. Granger took over as the new landlady."

"Hmm." There was nothing but pure doubt in that slow drawl.

"Am I speaking to the tenant?" Anna asked, it hadn't escaped her attention that the other person was yet to volunteer any information about herself. Heck, she couldn't tell if she was talking to a younger or older womxn. The voice on the other side of the phone was pleasant sounding, but there was a strange quality to it that made it hard to tell the age of the receiver.

"Yes, you're speaking to Dr. Susan Parker. You may address me as Dr. Parker." The voice said firmly. Anna tried to come up with a suitable mental image; she imagined a womxn in her forties, but having a youthful appearance.

"Dr. Parker, as I was asking, would it be convenient for me and my client to come over today for the general inspection of the place?" Anna asked.

Dr. Parker muttered something unintelligible, Anna imagined her cupping the end of the telephone and saying something to someone besides her; a spouse maybe.

"Alright, your timing isn't so inconvenient." She answered in a sardonic tone. "We'll be expecting you."

Dr. Parker hung up immediately but Anna was still frowning at her word choice. What did she mean by we?

Anna forced herself not to linger on it anymore, she focused her attention on the two womxns before her and lifted the corner of her lips in a robotic smile. "Good news, the tenant says that we can come over today. Everything is falling into place now, don't you agree?"

Beth offered up polite laughter at that but she didn't understand that Anna wasn't joking at all. The three of them were going to go on this trip, see the house and hopefully, the tenants would be stubborn sons of bitches who would refuse to settle quietly and move out. If Anna could help it, she was going to stop Beth from making the mistake of a lifetime today. The thought was as pleasing as punch.

∗∗∗

The day was certainly turning out to be one for surprises for Dr. Susan Parker; first, Simon was starting to show signs of descending into the out of body trip. She'd been trying to put him under for days but it had finally worked. Now, it might be interrupted because of the sudden guests they were having over.

Guests. Susan's lips curled down in a small frown; they weren't guests, they were more like intruders. She'd chosen this specific house to rent in Margate because of how private the community was. She could carry out her research and work without being interrupted; there were no nosy neighbours trying to stick their noses into her business. She hadn't been bothered much when the old landlady passed away and the property was passed off to a new landlady, up until now, Susan hadn't heard a peep from the new landlady. Not until now – and the horrible timing too.

She couldn't predict how long that Simon would be immersed in the psychedelic trip and the new landlady would be coming with her lawyer and god knew who else, they might demand a tour of the place too. How would she keep them away from here?

The other option would be to wake him up but it had taken her so much to get him under. It might be risky to wake him up; there was no telling how far he was gone.

She walked out of the room and found the other ladies in the back-yard garden where they often spent the day. For a moment, she just stood, half leaning against the sliding doors and observing them.

"Susie!" The younger womxn beckoned with a wave. "Why are you standing there?"

"The new landlady is coming to have a look today." She announced. The two womxns exchanged looks, wariness blooming in their gazes.

"What? The timing isn't convenient at all."

"What shall we do?"

"What do you need us to do?"

Susan cleared her throat, cutting through the panic rising. She was a little panicked herself but she couldn't afford to dwell on that. "Here's what we're going to do…"

CHAPTER SEVEN

Anna supposed that she should be offended by the surprise in Carrie's tone but she didn't really care. "Is there a problem with my car?" She asked, only to be polite, she didn't give a rat's ass about this womxn's opinion of her car.

Carrie snorted rudely. "It's a nice looking car, you'd think that the owner would be more fun loving but isn't that the problem with you lawyers?"

Beth gasped audibly in surprise. She didn't go as far as chastising Carrie publicly. She forced a smile on her face. "Please don't mind what Carrie says, she doesn't have much care for sugarcoating her true thoughts about something."

It must have been a trait that Beth once admired about her girlfriend, Anna could tell. It likely exasperated her now. She couldn't help but wonder how many times that Carrie had been rude to Beth's friends and family and how many times that Beth had had to excuse her behaviour with quirkiness.

Anna's car in question was a convertible that she'd gotten for herself years ago when she as first promoted. She didn't own plenty things that she was particularly attached to but she did like her car.

"It's alright." Anna said in response to Beth's apology.

She walked to the car and got into the driver's seat. Despite Carrie's sarcastic comment Anna could tell that she was impressed by the car as she hurried to the front seat, relegating Beth to the back of the car. Anna bit her lip, knowing that there was no way get Carrie to switch seats with Beth without being too obvious. She started the car and pulled out of the parking lot.

The awkward silence in the car was almost suffocating. Not a single word had been spoken by any of them in the car. Anna wasn't the greatest conversationalist in the world so she didn't even attempt to make small talk. She instead chose to make eye contact with Beth through the rearview mirror every few minutes. Beth who was quiet and seemingly lost in her thoughts.

On the other hand, Carrie made no attempt to hide her displeasure, sighing and grunting unintelligibly every now and then. Anna was tempted to turn on the radio to drown out her sighs.

Carrie was thinking of how to make her escape. Every few minutes that passed was another minute from her freedom. She didn't like that Beth was trying to force her into committing to this fucking house, hell, it seemed to her that Beth was being too obsessive; she'd move them to fucking Antarctica if she could just so that she could watch Carrie's every move.

Sure, Carrie was going to get a house of this whole situation if she played her cards right but she couldn't help but wonder how she'd gotten herself into this mess in the first place. She remembered meeting Beth two years ago. Despite the fact that Beth liked to tell her friends the oh so romantic story of how she'd met Carrie's eyes at a pub.

The actual events were kind of a blur to Carrie, maybe because she'd been a little drunk that night. True, their eyes had indeed met. The pub was tame in comparison to the usual nightclubs that Carrie frequented but that night, she'd left the gallery opening of a friend earlier than planned. Everyone knew that artists had the worst career luck; it was difficult to attain the level of success that many of them craved. Back then Carrie had been suffering the worst kind of luck and dealing with a creative block, she hadn't painted anything in months and attending that opening that night, pretending to be happy for her friend even though she wanted to claw at all the displayed art. She'd made up an excuse about an emergency and bolted out of the gallery before she choked on her jealousy. She'd walked for ten minutes, searching for the closest pub to wander in and drink her woes away.

That was how she met Beth; a young successful womxn celebrating closing out a deal with a C list celebrity. Beth too had been out with some friends. Carrie had been well buzzed when she noticed Beth. Carrie and Beth's eye had met then and Carrie wouldn't lie, she'd been a little taken aback by Beth's beauty. That night she'd been wearing a black sleeveless dress that hugged her figure well. Carrie had always had a thing for curvy womxns.

She'd noticed the way Beth's eyes lingered on her too; too long to be considered curiosity. She'd been admiring Carrie too. Carrie, in simple terms, had been thinking of shagging her. That was it, leaving with a beautiful womxn on her arm and waking up with her in bed would have been just the thing to get Carrie in a much better mood. Especially when Beth commanded the attention of half of the room; even though she seemed oblivious to the effect she had on her admirers. That was what Beth was supposed to be; an uncomplicated fuck.

Except, Carrie had found her a little refreshing from her usual lovers. Beth was sweet, annoyingly so. In the beginning, it had been endearing; Carrie's jadedness paired with Beth's untouched optimism. Carrie had liked her. Then like she usually did, she'd gotten bored but it had been too late by then. Beth was attached and Carrie was attached to the financial safety that Beth was. Beth was richer than anybody else Carrie had ever been with and generous too; lavishing Carrie with expensive gifts. She became Carrie's safety net.

So the charade of a relationship continued – only made known to one of them – and here they were, two years into it and Carrie was sick of it. Sick of having to commit, to promise unending devotion just to keep Beth's anxieties at ease. Like now.

She'd tried to communicate her displeasure by sighing heavily and mumbling but then that darned lawyer had turned on the radio, commenting that she just absolutely needed to hear the news. If Carrie didn't know better, she might think that Anna Fenwick was the devil. She shot Anna a glare from the corner of her eyes but the womxn's eyes were fixed ahead on the road. Carrie shook her head. Of course, Beth had found the most unshakeable womxn in the world.

Carrie prided herself on being unbearable, she'd learnt early in life that it was the only way that she would ever be heard. So she yelled, she made caustic and sarcastic remarks, she was like a Hollywood actor but on steroids with all the theatrics she put up on a daily basis. It was a great tactic that usually worked on most people that Carrie knew but Anna Fenwick was ostensibly immovable and infuriating.

She sighed again and Anna's eyes left the road for a quick second, met Carrie's – Carrie could have sworn that the glint in them was mischief swimming in their depths as she reached out and turned up the volume up a notch. Carrie gritted her teeth and winced, she touched a hand to her head. She was still hungover from last night. *I shouldn't have drunk so much with Tiff,* She thought with a silent groan. She hadn't even had the chance to take an advil.

Carrie looked out the window with a frown. The car hit a speed pump and her head throbbed with sharp pain. She was starting to feel woozy. If they didn't stop any time soon, Carrie thought she might puke all over Anna Fenwick's leather seats.

She inhaled a breath and another, the car zoomed past a service station. An idea suddenly occurred to Carrie and she would have smiled if her head didn't pound with a furious intensity.

She groaned aloud this time, loud enough to be heard above the radio. She heard Beth sit up a little straighter.

"Car, what's the problem?" Beth asked with concern in her voice like Carrie predicted that she would.

"I don't feel so good, car sickness." She said.

Anna's gave her a cursory glance. She looked more suspicious than concerned. For a second, Carrie wondered why this womxn seemed to hate her even though they just met today. And for once, Carrie wasn't exaggerating. There was a way that Anna had been looking at her for the past hour; with suspicion and strong dislike – which was very strange seeing as Carrie had been perfectly polite – except in the instances that Anna had clearly tried to prevent the joint ownership deal from becoming a reality.

"Car sick?" Beth echoed with some incredulity. She clearly couldn't recall much instances that Carrie had been car sick but she leaned forward to take a look at Carrie's face and there was no mistaking the green tint of her face. She was sweating despite the coolness of the car.

"I think you need to pull over." Beth told Anna.

"There's a service station just ahead." Anna said in that efficient way of hers.

One minute later, Anna was pulling up into the service station and killing the engine of the car. Carrie barely waited, she pushed open the car door and burst out into open air. She gulped it in greedily. The air wasn't so clear, there was the strong, sharp smell of petrol and grease.

Beth got out of the car and headed after Carrie.

"Carrie, wait up." Beth was saying. Very likely hobbling on the kitten heels she was wearing. Beth was hopeless when it came to heeled shoes — that was one of the first disappointments of their relationship. Carrie had discovered that Beth wasn't the seductive siren she'd met at the pub. She didn't like dressing up like Carrie loved to, comfortable in more casual clothes.

Carrie didn't wait for Beth to reach her. She immediately dashed into the mart. Her head spun as she pushed open the doors to enter into the mart.

It was hot inside, clearly the air conditioning wasn't working. There was a young man with the most distinctive looking moustache behind the counter, flipping through an issue of British fashion magazine. He briefly raised his head up at the sound of the door but he immediately went back to reading his magazine.

Carrie glanced around. The mart was as good as dead, more than half of the aisle shelves were empty. And when she walked past a shelf, she caught graffiti on it. She walked up to the cashier and slammed a fist on the counter. Her head was still spinning and she was beginning to think she might puke all over the tiles if she didn't get to a restroom soon.

"Where's the restroom?" She asked.

Something like wariness flashed in the eyes of the cashier, he seemed to assess her for a moment, likely trying to detect if she was some kind of criminal or something. His assessment was just a few seconds but to Carrie, it felt like an eternity. In the end, he frowned.

"You have to buy something. It's only for customers." He said sourly.

Carrie shot him a venomous glare and leaned in close until he shrank back. "Where. Is. The. Fucking. Bathroom?" She exploded.

He pointed a shaky finger at a door on the right and she hurriedly dashed into it, leaving the door open.

She hurried into the nearest stall and threw up into the toilet bowl, her free hand gripping the edge. She continued to dry heave for a full minutes before she staggered to her feet and headed to the sink to wash her face. She pulled out her phone from her purse and called Tiff.

Tiff picked up on the third ring. "Carrie?" She sounded surprised. It was actually unusual for Carrie to call her.

Their relationship was purely physical, no strings attached. Carrie came over on their planned days but outside that, there was little to no communication between the two of them.

"Just stay on the phone with me and agree with everything I say." Carrie told her with a tinge of warning in her voice. She had to make this believable to Beth, that was the only way she was getting out of this situation.

And Tiff had the habit of being mischievous. Sometimes, Carrie didn't trust her.

Carrie walked out of the restroom and almost right into Beth whose eyes were saucer wide with concern.

"Car, are you alright?" She asked, moving to touch a hand to Carrie's head.

Carrie held up a finger to stop her and gestured at the phone. Beth immediately caught on and took a step back.

Carrie supposed that she should have felt guilty, maybe a little bit of it, anything to show that she cared about lying to Beth. She didn't though, maybe one day she might let Beth know how she really felt about her but today wasn't that day.

"Oh, right... I'm actually in the middle an impromptu trip with my girlfriend..." Carrie said into the phone speaker, feigning seriousness.

On the other end, Tiff gave a derisive snort. "Bragging in my face, aren't we?"

Carrie fought to keep her face passive, infusing the right amount of frustration in her face — as if she gave a damn about missing this trip.

"Come back? But..." She trailed off deliberately again. She saw that Beth was hanging on to her every word.

"I want to make you come." Tiff said. There was that usual mischief thick in the drawl of her voice. Carrie almost lost it there and then.

"Alright, I'll be right there. Yeah, see you soon." Carrie finished. She didn't wait to hear Tiff's reply, she hung up.

By now, Beth was looking crestfallen. She might be plenty of things;

naive, too fricking optimistic for her own good but she wasn't stupid. She had likely pieced together most of the conversation.

"Got a call in there." Carrie began stiffly, still putting up the front of disappointed girlfriend. "They're asking me to come in and kiss the ass of some hotshot, new gallery owner. Henri says that I could have a real chance of having some of my old stuff featured."

Even though she had been on the phone with Tiff. Henri did actually exist and they were Carrie's 'manager' in the loosest sense of the word. They were Carrie's oldest and probably only friend. The two of them had been childhood friends, growing up in the same dysfunctional situation and environment.

Henri had been the first to get out of their abusive, homophobic parents' home. They had gone to university and even graduated, studying Art History. Carrie had gone on to do her own thing; mostly illegal — just anything she could do to survive. She'd been high most of the time too and it was during that period that she began to paint; almost obsessively and excessively. She had created some of the most disturbing material. Back then, Carrie hadn't any desire of being some famous artist, she had only painted because it was a medium of expressing thoughts and feelings that she couldn't otherwise express publicly.

It was Henri; who was fresh out of university and without a job that thought she was good, enough that painting could be more than a hobby and more of a career. They had some contacts from uni and everything had kind of snowballed from there. Carrie had started getting some spotlight for her work and Henri unofficially managed her in the sense that there was no legal paperwork signed, they made sure she got her art sold and they took a reasonable cut of her earnings.

Years later, Henri had branched out to managing more than Carrie and she'd started to make less and less art. Still, they didn't chuck her to the streets, Henri still encouraged her. So, yes, they were more of a friend to Carrie than anyone else.

In fact, she almost felt guilty using their name as a lie to Beth but it was the only way that Beth would believe her. Because she happened to also like Henri.

"Henri?" Beth asked. She didn't seem suspicious per se, just surprised. Carrie bet that she was thinking of how supportive Henri was of their relationship. They were the last person she'd expect to interrupt their trip for business.

"Hold on to this one, Car, she's a good one." They'd often talk about Beth to Carrie. Over the years, Carrie had gotten sick of it too. When she'd first introduced Henri to Beth, it was because Beth hadn't stopped nagging that she'd never met any of Carrie's friends. Carrie had thought that it would be one big colossal joke to introduce the two to each other. She thought that Henri might get the joke too; Beth was the type of person that they had grown up making fun of — rich, uptight kids.

But Henri had immediately taken a liking to Beth, much to Carrie's chagrin.

"They sounded apologetic on the phone but this isn't something I can miss." Carrie said flatly, walking past Beth and past an aisle of feminine products. She noticed that it was one of the few shelves in the store that was properly stocked.

"But on the trip, we were supposed to look at the house together." Beth sounded so crestfallen that Carrie felt some long forgotten flicker of feelings for her.

Sometimes, she wondered why she didn't just cut Beth loose and let her go. Apart from the obvious of course. A better womxn would be grateful for all Beth had done for her, a better womxn might try all her best to love Beth the way that she deserved. But Carrie wasn't exactly a better person.

The cashier's gaze flicked up as she came into his line of sight. He sent her a glower that she pretended not to see. She walked out the door with Beth in tow.

"Sorry, Beth," Carrie said, not at all sounding sorry. "You said it yourself, it's Henri. They rarely ever interrupt us but this time, it has to be really urgent."

She let a little bit of frustration shine through in her voice, "This is my career we're talking about Beth. We can't all be you, having the privilege not to think about money for the rest of our lives."

Beth recoiled, clearly stung. Carrie felt that familiar voice whispering in her ears, telling her to push Beth harder. It was so easy to make Beth feel terrible about herself, she was so insecure that she took every verbal beat down lying, she even cried. It was too bad for her that Carrie had one hell of a mean streak.

"It's not like that, Car, I care about your work." She protested.

Carrie rolled her eyes. "Sure you do. When was the last time you saw me paint?"

Beth parted her lips to speak but no words came out. She didn't have an answer to that. Her cheeks were flushed red, a telltale sign of embarrassment. She was going to start crying soon.

"There we have it. You don't know, because you don't care." She fired.

Beth was openly crying now, a few tears streaking down her cheek. She cried prettily, not making a single sound. Maybe that was why Carrie liked to poke her too much, because, goodness, she'd never met anyone who managed to make crying look pretty.

Carrie left her standing there and walked to the car where the lawyer was still seated inside, waiting for them. Carrie opened the door and entered.

She waited a beat, for the devastatingly cold Anna Fenwick to say something. Carrie had noticed her watching them, not even making an attempt to pretend otherwise. There was something stern in the set of her jaw, as if she was biting back words. But the look cleared almost immediately Carrie saw it and she was left thinking that she'd imagined it.

Carrie looked stubbornly ahead.

"Beth got you a few things while you were in there." The lawyer said after a beat of silence, jerking her head at the white paper bag on the floor of Carrie's seat. Oh, so that was what Carrie had been brushing her leg against.

She picked it up and pulled out a sandwich, a bottle of water and painkillers. She uncapped the bottle and drank, gulping the water. She wiped a few dribbles of water down her chin.

Then she popped several pills into her mouth and swallowed them. Again, she expected Anna Fenwick to say something, to chide her. Carrie was itching more than anything to fight this womxn too. She couldn't stand her smug looks and how she thought she knew everything.

This whole trip was her fault, if only she'd just let Beth sign the joint ownership papers then they wouldn't be in this situation. The both of them miserable; Carrie miserable because she had to go on this trip and Beth miserable because she wasn't getting what she wanted.

But as usual, Anna Fenwick was silent, still so. She didn't drum on the steering wheel like other people might do, neither did she jiggle a foot. She just sat still, it made it hard for Carrie to guess what she was thinking.

A few minutes later, Beth entered the car and Anna began to drive again, no questions asked.

"We're near Dartford, can you let me off when we're there?" Carrie asked.

She hated the way that the lawyer's eyes sought out Beth's in the rear-view mirror, as if she was asking for permission. As if Carrie was Beth's ward and incapable of making her own choices.

"Car..." Beth tried again.

With a fury that surprised even her, Carrie snapped, "Don't, Beth. Don't make this harder than it should be."

"I have to meet Henri at the gallery. It's not something you can talk me out of so please stop trying."

That shut Beth up immediately. Carrie thought she heard a muffled squeak from the back. If Anna Fenwick heard, she didn't let it show on her face.

When they were nearing Dartford, Anna pulled the car over to the side of the road to let Carrie out.

Carrie grabbed the sandwich bag. She didn't even deign Beth with a full goodbye.

"Let me know how it goes, if you two end up going." She said over her shoulder and then she was gone, slamming the door harder than necessary, whether as some kind of final revenge against the cold Anna Fenwick or to frighten Beth even further, Carrie wasn't so sure.

Then again, she wasn't sure of half of the things that she usually did.

***

That fucking artist.

Anna didn't get the urge to name-call somebody often, in fact, she was usually mild towards people and she'd definitely never met someone that she hated immediately. Congratulations to Carrie for breaking that record.

Fuck apathy, Anna couldn't stay cold and detached when Beth was crying in the backseat. She came out of the car and opened the door to enter the backseat.

The full sight of Beth made her heart clench in her chest. She sat stiffly, trying to wipe away the tears that were falling, the action was stubborn, frustrated, echoing someone who was used to their partner making them cry often. There was a look of incredulous disbelief on Beth's face, as if she didn't believe that she was crying over Carrie again.

"I'm so sorry for Carrie's rude manners. She isn't usually like that." Beth finally said.

Anna held back an amused snort, she didn't want to offend Beth more. She didn't need a seer to tell her that Carrie was likely a hundred percent nasty all of the time. She'd observed enough of her.

"Hey, you know what they say, three is a crowd." Anna joked — or tried to. Except, she had no delivery and the words came out flat.

She caught Beth's embarrassed wince and almost echoed the action herself.

"That was the wrong thing to say. Sorry, I'm not very good with jokes. Or making people feel better about themselves." Anna said, admitting the truth out loud for the first time in her life. She half expected Beth to laugh mockingly at her.

Who the hell didn't know how to make jokes?

"I suppose they don't teach that in law school. How to make your clients feel at ease 101," Beth replied with a half smile.

She was joking. Anna let herself expel a tiny sigh of relief, most times she often didn't know what to say and usually ended up saying the wrong thing.

There was a beat of silence between them. Beth was dabbing at her cheeks with tissue.

"I'm sorry." Anna said. She wasn't apologising for Carrie or even because it seemed like the kind of thing people said to other people who cried. She was truly sorry that a womxn like Beth would end up with the cruellest partner. It didn't seem fair at all.

Beth gave a careless shrug. "I'll be alright."

She leaned back in the seat and shook her head from side to side, a forced smile on her face. "Maybe we should go back… I mean, there's no use going ahead with this trip. Carrie and I were supposed to see the house together and now that she's gone." Beth shrugged again, trying to convey nonchalance. "I don't want to waste your time anymore, Miss Fenwick."

"Anna." Anna said. "You can call me Anna."

Beth looked a little taken aback but she smiled, this one a little more genuine than the last one.

"Right, Anna. We'll have to postpone this trip for a later day when Carrie can come with us." Beth said.

So you mean never? Anna thought. She didn't even believe that Carrie had received a phone call. She was being flaky, doing anything she could to avoid committing to Beth. Anna understood that it was a big decision to own a house together, it was definitely something that required careful consideration. But from the looks of things, Beth and Carrie had been together for years. Enough time for a couple to think of making serious commitments together. Not running away from it.

Anna didn't want Beth to make a mistake though. She needed to see the gravity of the situation; preferably that Carrie was a toxic partner but she would gladly settle for changing Beth's mind about sharing the property with Carrie.

"It's a tricky situation though," Anna began, choosing her words carefully. "This trip is a necessary legal step. You have to speed things up if you want to take any action at all. Notices must be given out at appropriate times or a lawsuit could come back to bite you." She was lying through her straight white teeth. For a brief moment, she felt a pang of guilt, hating that she was lying to Beth but resolve caused her spine to straighten.

She was trying to help Beth and that was all.

As usual, when most people heard the word, legal, they sat up straight and Beth was no exception.

"Oh, I don't want anything to be up for contention. And I trust you. I'm in your hands." Beth said firmly, gazing at Anna with clear blue eyes.

Anna tried to ignore how Beth's trust made her feel warmth in her chest. She needed to stay completely logical to handle this. It seemed that Beth enjoyed decisions being made for her, she was hesitant about taking matters into her own hands. Anna wondered how much of that insecurity could be traced back to Carrie.

"Good. And Beth?"

"Hm?" Anna wondered if Beth realised that this was the first time that Anna had addressed her by the nickname that she'd offered.

"Come sit in the front. I'm not a cabbie."

Beth laughed at that, the sound carefree in a way that made Anna want to bottle up the sound for herself.

Anna couldn't stop staring at her for a long moment, taking in her face. The dotted freckles on her cheek. The curve of her lips, happier than Anna had seen her in the past hours. Anna knew that Beth was beautiful, she'd taken note of it the moment she'd seen her mid row with Carrie in her usual clinical way. Now she was seeing that beauty in a different light. A brighter one now that she was smiling.

Happy Beth was a lethal womxn and she didn't even know it.

CHAPTER *EIGHT*

Beth had kicked off her shoes and was sitting with her legs crossed; one over the other. There was none of that lingering sadness in her eyes. For the past half hour, they'd done nothing but talk. Anna had thought that she didn't like small talk; she'd always despised how people traded niceties by talking about the weather or some other stuff like that, pretending as if it was insightful information instead. But with Beth, it was different, every word said was meaningful, a further insight into the kind of person that Beth was. In the past thirty minutes, Anna had discovered plenty of things about her; that she didn't like her food cold, that she wore socks to bed and most interesting of all, that she'd majored in Plant Biology in university. She knew that Beth managed real estate and that it was a family business so she'd expected that Beth would have studied business in college or something similar.

She mentioned it again.

"Why plant biology though?" Anna had to ask, she sensed a childhood incentive coming up. She was struck by her growing desire to know everything that there was to know about Beth.

She wanted to make her smile, to make a thousand jokes that would coax that laughter from her. Some distant part of her mind warned her against getting so easily attached, because that was what was going on here; Anna already enjoyed Beth's company and the lines were beginning to blur. It seemed like the both of them were deliberately ignoring that the two of them weren't two friends out on a road trip, they had a lawyer-client relationship. It might take Anna a few days tops to convince Beth not to pursue the house in Margate and to perhaps hold off joint ownership. Once this was done, they would go back to being strangers and Anna might never see her again, maybe they might bump into each other in the city, they might say hi to each other, offer a distant smile but that would be all. Beth might still be with Carrie and Anna… well, Anna would still be alone.

She ought to be setting the priorities straight, not making friends with her clients. It's unprofessional, her head warned. But forget about being a professional, Anna didn't care; she couldn't remember ever connecting with someone like this, ever. She may as well enjoy it before it is over.

Beth was silent for a second in contemplation, Anna could tell that she was mulling over whether to trust Anna with the story or not.

"It's silly." Beth said half heartedly.

"No, it's not." Anna immediately countered.

Beth wore an amused look on her face. "You can't know that, you haven't even heard the story yet."

"I don't think there's anything silly about how you came to discover something that grew into a passion for you. I've always envied people who have these stories to tell about why they chose a career path, for some of us; it's a little less cold. There was no epiphany that made me go, yes, I want to become a lawyer, and this is what I want to do for the rest of my life." Anna explained. She wasn't much of a talker, her favourite thing to do was listening – from an early age, most people had thought it weird that Anna didn't want to chat away like other kids her age did. She would sit in front of the telly, watching the news with her mother. Anna would rather hear other people's stories than talk about her own, simply because there was nothing to tell. She wasn't passionate about a lot of stuff. In fact, she didn't care much about things. In school, she'd been a diligent student, doing as she was told and excelling. When the time had come for her to decide what to do in university, she'd gone with Law because her mother was one. Anna liked life just fine; it wasn't excellent by any means but it was okay and she was content with living like that, with having no passions.

"How did you know you wanted to be a lawyer?" Beth asked incredulously. She clearly didn't believe that Anna didn't have a story similar to hers.

Anna shrugged, she zoned out for a second, realising that in less than fifty minutes, they would be getting to Margate. She didn't understand why the thought filled her with so much fright. Her hands clenched around the steering wheel and she forced herself to take a deep breath and answer Beth's question calmly.

"I didn't." She replied.

Beth sat up a little straighter. Anna hated that she was driving; she was usually a careful driver, keeping her hands steadily on the wheel and keeping her eyes solely on the road. The statistics for road accidents were too high that she was ultra careful. But she wished it wasn't so, so that she could drink her fill of the sight of Beth, that she could give her the rapt attention that she was deserving of.

"That's a lie." Beth said.

"I wouldn't lie to you." Anna said with an intensity that shocked her. That statement too was a lie of sorts, Anna hated to lie to Beth but her lie was the only reason that they were still on this trip. She wondered how Beth would feel if she found out the truth, if she would think that Anna pitied her.

Stop daydreaming, she chided herself. "I decided to become a property lawyer because my mother was one. See, no passionate story of how I was determined to change the justice system of the country."

"Was?" Beth asked softly. Most people would have ignored that.

"Yeah. She passed two years ago, heart attack."

"I'm sorry, Anna. You must miss her a lot." Beth said.

Anna did miss her mother, she was a lot like her, gruff and more than a little awkward when it came to social interactions. It had always been her and Anna. It was a surprise that she'd married Anna's father, a bubbly, extroverted man. It was another surprise that Anna hadn't inherited any of that bubbly persona. She was her mother's daughter through and through.

"I do miss her."

"I'm allergic to dogs." Beth said.

Anna cast her a brief sideways look, wondering what she was hinting at. Beth giggled at the clear confusion that must have been written all over Anna's face.

"You asked for my childhood epiphany and I'm telling you."

"I'm listening." Anna said.

At that, Beth looked at Anna strange, a mix of realisation and something else – awe? It was hard to tell when Anna's eyes couldn't leave the road for more than three seconds tops.

"Yeah, you are." She said softly.

"The story about the dogs." Anna urged her on.

"Right. I was allergic as a kid. I went through this phase of wanting to get a pet so bad as a kid, my parents obviously couldn't get me a dog because I was allergic nor a cat because my mom was allergic. There were other pet options but I didn't want a hamster – I was afraid of them back then. So as a little kid, all your options are pretty much limited to dogs or cats and I couldn't get any of them."

"All the other kids my age had pets of their own, they'd talk about it during recess and I was sooo jealous of them." Beth laughed. "Then one day, we were taught about plants and our teacher gave an assignment to plant seeds and grow them for about three weeks, we were given a bunch of other instructions too."

"Seeing that first leaf sprout up from the dirt pot I'd put it in is probably still one of the best things that has ever happened to me. I was so proud. I didn't stop with just that assignment, I looked into other kinds of fun stuff I could plant by myself, my parents were relieved that I finally laid off talking about the dog abut I think they were a little scared of my new obsession, I begged them to let me turn our backyard into a small garden. By the time I was seventeen, I already had a mini farm of my own."

Anna smiled, she imagined a headstrong Beth, refusing to yield to her parents. The womxn sitting next to her was still the same way; nurturing and confident, even though the latter had taken a beating too many times to count.

"Why didn't you do anything with your degree in plant biology?" Anna asked, she regretted her question when Beth's smile wiped off her face clean and a frown took its place. Sometimes, Anna had to constantly remind herself that just because she'd been lucky to have understanding parents, it didn't mean that others had the same luck. She was often surprised when other people spoke of how awful their parents were, she found it hard to phantom that not all parents loved and supported her children the way hers had.

She remembered announcing to her parents that she was going to study law, as early as twelve. During career week at school when her teacher had brought in a few professionals to come and talk to them. She'd declared at the end of the day that she was going to be a lawyer because her mother was one.

"Anna, love, you know that you don't have to do the same thing that I do, right?" Her mother had asked with that usual patient expression on her face, the one that made her look untouchable and the one that Anna usually mimicked.

"I know that." She'd answered. Back then, she'd been perfectly logical, thinking that selecting a career was exactly like choosing what to eat. There was no use considering irrelevant details like passion.

She was debating that stance now – she loved the passion that Beth had, it sparkled in the blue of her eyes and it made her look as if she was glowing.

"Family business, remember?"

For someone who spoke of passion, her tone was a little lacking to Anna. "And? You went through hell to get your wish to major in Plant Biology and you're telling me that you never fought for your degree to be used?" Anna couldn't keep the skeptically from her voice. For a second she wondered if she'd taken it too and upset Beth but she shook off the thought. Beth needed to be challenged, not sitting down and taking notes from anybody. Was it Carrie who had made her this way?

Beth didn't answer at first and when a full minute passed, Anna thought she wouldn't. Even kindhearted Beth may have her own limits.

"It wasn't even something I considered, I'd had the most freedom in college than I had in my entire life, you should have seen me back then." Beth said slowly, her voice a little distant in a way that told Anna that she was lost in her thoughts. She suddenly smiled. "I was the wildest."

"Really?" Anna deadpanned.

Beth laughed. "I was. I think it was because I knew that after college, I'd have to go back to how things were; my whole life being dictated by my family. So I had the best years of my life abroad and came back here to settle. Now that you mention it, I wonder how different things would be right now if I had dared to broach the subject with them." She gave a morose shrug. "I guess we'll never know." She added.

Anna was thinking that it might not be too late for that; to start over.

Then she shook her head to herself wondering when she became so optimistic.

"So that's how it's going to be forever?" Anna couldn't help but ask, she needed to know that Beth hadn't given up on everything.

Beth smiled bashfully. "In our apartment, there's a hothouse where I grow and sell carnivorous plants. It's absolutely beautiful in there."

Anna didn't know much about plants, in fact, she couldn't differentiate one from the other. But she found herself nodding at the imagery, absolutely believing Beth.

'Have you got any plants of your own? I know that animals aren't all the rage now, some people are plant mums." Beth asked.

Anna couldn't help it, she laughed. "Maybe I should get one. What would you recommend?" She could tell by the way Beth smiled that she was pleased. "I'll gift you something. It's the least I can do for putting you through this trouble."

Anna wasn't smiling anymore. "Beth, I'm your solicitor – I work for you. Trust me, you aren't making me do anything I don't want to do in the slightest."

But Beth wasn't really listening. "I've really troubled you today, and on top of it Carrie has been totally weird." She turned a little in her seat so that she was facing Anna.

"What do you think I should do about her? She's clearly frightened by this trip."

It was getting harder and harder for Anna to keep her true thoughts about Carrie to herself. Anna was one more hairsbreadth from snapping and telling Beth everything. She was trying not to be obnoxious and pushy but it was starting to infuriate her how much Beth avoided real facts and made excuses to suit the narrative that she wanted.

"Frightened? She's not a kid, Beth, she's an adult in a consenting relationship with another adult. She doesn't get to run away because she's frightened. That's not what adults do." Anna tried to say lightly.

"Are you in a relationship, Anna?" Beth asked.

"My last relationship ended over a year ago." Anna answered. "My girlfriend and I decided that it was better to go our separate ways when she got a job in another city."

Anna could count the number of relationships she'd been in throughout her lifetime on one hand and she'd still have a couple of fingers left. She didn't like people easily and worse, most people didn't like her easily.

"Carrie and I have been together for more than two years and I know her more than I know myself. She's been through some tough stuff and I just try to protect her because nobody has ever been there for her like that before." Beth said. "I want her to know that I love her and that I'm willing to do anything for her. I want to coax her out of that shell that she's hiding in."

It might be considered rude if Anna told Beth that the only shell that she was hiding in was one of self-absorption.

"Carrie can be incapable of seeing the bigger picture. When I first told her about the house in Margate, she all but told me to let it burn to the ground."

Now, that would have been something. If only Beth wasn't consumed with the desire to fix what she thought was wrong with her relationship, despite the fact that none of it was her fault.

"But she's come around to owning the house together. I know she'll love the place when she sees it, I just need to get her to come with me." Beth continued. "Maybe if you tell her that it's some sort of legal requirement for the two of us to visit, maybe then she'll come."

Anna couldn't tell her that it was the same excuse that she'd used on Beth. But she didn't interrupt, with every word, Beth grew more animated. Her cheeks were flushed and her eye sparkled. Anna resisted the urge to tell her how beautiful she looked.

"There has to be a way to trick her into coming with us."

Anna shook her head, "Beth, that's how you talk about getting a cat to the vet."

***

Carrie felt the biggest burden lifted up from her shoulder the moment that she stepped into the train station.

"Fucking finally," She muttered under her breath, she shook her head, imagining herself back in that cramped car with Beth's hopes hanging in the stilted air and so suffocating. Sometimes she wondered why Beth wasn't more carefree; she was rich, likely had a trust fund from dearest daddy and mummy and she didn't even have to do anything to work for it. She could relax, take a few holidays around the world – like Carrie had suggested too many times to count. That was the relationship that Carrie had signed up for; jetting around the world, renting expensive holiday villas around the world and just having fun. Beth had refused though, she didn't understand why they needed to take a vacation in the middle of January.

"There's nothing to celebrate." She would say.

Carrie usually threw up her hands in exasperation and say, "Holidays aren't about celebrating, Beth, they're about having fun, winding down from all the stress and shit of live; you know, getting wasted on beaches, partying all night long and getting our tans on. That is what holidays are all about."

Except, all of Carrie's attempts at persuasion had fallen on deaf ears. None of the things that Carrie had mentioned seemed to remotely excite Beth. She didn't like parties much – occasionally she would go out with Carrie and her friends but she didn't enjoy the club scene at all. Beth's idea of fun was lying in the house in sweatpants and watching highly rated TV series or tending to her plants. Maybe if Beth had listened to Carrie in the first place, then they wouldn't be in this situation; she'd gotten it in her head that if she moved them to the middle of freaking nowhere then all would be fine in their relationship.

Carrie snorted as she waited for her train to arrive, she'd never heard a more foolish idea. She might be into moving if it was some fucking mansion in Barbados, not the middle of nowhere in Kent.

Carrie fiddled with the pack of cigarettes she'd bought and took out a lighter from her pocket. She carried the lighter everywhere – it had once belonged to her mother – a few minutes later, her train arrived and she immediately got on it.

She took a seat on the right and continued to fiddle with her lighter. She was going to get wasted. She definitely deserved it after the terrible morning that she'd had.

***

"What do you mean by taking a cat to the vet?" Beth asked, she supposed that she should have been offended by Anna's implications, she was being subtle, yes but Beth wasn't stupid. At least she only seemed to lose all sense of reasoning when it came to Carrie.

She couldn't blame Anna for the advice; because Anna didn't know Carrie. She didn't know how she'd come into Beth's life at a moment where things were the most bleak for her.

It was true what Beth had told Anna; that she'd barely fought to put that Plant Biology degree to use, she'd been so glad to see her parents even though her relationship with them was shaky in more than one way. America had been fun but she'd been a different Beth, desperate to savor all the last bits of freedom. That Beth wasn't the real her; the real Beth had been very afraid and hid all that fear behind a mask of cocky bravado. So when she'd returned home, she hadn't even fought with her parents, she'd gracefully slipped back into her old life of taking orders from them, letting them dictate what she was going to do with her life, who her friends were going to be.

She had begun to slowly wilt until that night she met Carrie. She'd been out with some of her cousins who wanted to hear all the adventures of America's Beth; they had swiftly realised that the British Beth was much more tamer, refusing to take shots with them because she had to meet with clients the next morning. But one cousin still lingered, Vanessa who kept trying to get Beth to dance and show them some 'American moves'. It was in that moment, as Beth struggled to get out of her cousin's grip that she met Carrie's eyes from across the pub. She'd known then that Carrie was going to save her; there was no missing the glimmer of interest in her eyes that night.

Carrie had swiftly intercepted, pretending to be Beth's old pal from school. When Vanessa had successfully quizzed Carrie to her satisfaction, she let the two of them be. This time, when Carrie bought her a shot, there had been a daring glint in her eyes and Beth had wanted nothing more than to prove her wrong. For a moment, Beth had felt like American Beth again; daring and wanting to impress a beautiful womxn.

Carrie made her feel that way and Beth would love her for it forever. She didn't expect Anna to understand it and she didn't try to explain it; half afraid that she would be mocked. To be fair though, Anna had been anything but mocking in the past hour. She was refreshingly honest in a way that many people might think was curt but Beth saw the sincerity shining in her eyes every time she spoke; even though she was blunt, she meant well and that was all that mattered to Beth. It also mattered that she made Beth laugh harder than anyone had in a while.

Beth liked her very much, maybe a little too much than was normal – she'd just met this womxn today and she was already discussing her relationship woes with her.

How pathetic can you get? A voice in her head mocked. Beth flinched, not because the words were cruel but because the voice in her head sounded awfully like Carrie's. Beth shook her head and forced herself to focus on Anna.

Anna was still carefully considering her answer, it seemed. In the end, she shook her head.

"I just don't think that you can condition another person like that, Beth. Carrie has to want to make this work, to go the extra mile in your relationship." She said carefully. Even though her voice was perfectly normal, Beth couldn't help but bristle on Carrie's behalf.

"Carrie is trying." Beth argued. How would she explain Carrie to Anna in a way that would be understood and not judged? She was torn between the urge to tell Anna everything about Carrie's troubled childhood and the urge to protect Carrie. Carrie hated to feel vulnerable more than anything else, she wouldn't like it if Beth spilled her secrets. On the other hand, Beth didn't often get the chance to talk about her relationship woes with other people.

Carrie had met her family on several occasions. Her cousins liked her, they thought she was the coolest, most sophisticated womxn. Carrie often met with Sophie; Beth's oldest cousin for tea. Her parents on the other hand would be more disappointed in Beth if they found out that her relationship wasn't what they thought it was.

Anna's eyes strayed from the road for a quick second to shoot Beth a look of deep amusement. Beth found herself thinking of how expressive Anna's eyes were; they were a grey that reminded her of a stormy sky. Beautiful, she thought.

"You're thinking of something," Beth said, forcing herself to focus on Anna rather than how attractive her lawyer was.

Anna shook her head.

"Come on, you have to tell me." Beth said with a teasing smile. She liked how even though Anna was staring ahead at the road, concentrating on driving, she was still paying Beth the most rapt attention; she didn't miss any frown, any tiny smile or look. Beth knew that she must be a very good lawyer; lawyers had to be in tune with all that kind of stuff, right?

When Anna said nothing, Beth said, "You're a good listener."

"What makes you think that?" Anna asked. Beth's eyes strayed to her hands on the steering wheel; her nails were painted black, not a single chip of the paint. Unlike Beth who often spent time biting her nails and ruining her manicure. Anna was calm and collected in a way so unlike Beth, in fact, she was calmer than anyone Beth had ever met; it spoke of a solid confidence in herself that Beth found herself envying a little.

"Even though you aren't looking at me, you still manage to make me feel heard – I don't feel like I'm talking to someone unresponsive." Beth answered, she wasn't sure if she was articulate enough but Anna nodded once, seeming to understand perfectly what she'd meant.

"All this talk of Carrie, you said you ended things with your last girlfriend over a year ago." Beth said. Beth didn't know why she'd felt relieved finding out that Anna was queer like her but she had. "Why? You could have done the long distance thing."

Anna didn't answer for a beat and Beth hurriedly added, "If it's okay for you to talk about."

"I think I can spare a few secrets." Anna said, shooting Beth a smirk that immediately faded. "I'm not a very good at communication."

"Could have fooled me," Beth said and meant it. "You're talking to me just fine."

A look flashed on Anna's face, too quick for Beth to decipher. If she had to guess, she might have named it insecurity? Except, she couldn't guess what Anna was insecure about. Those things run deeper than the surface, she reminded herself. Nobody could have guessed all those years ago that Beth was depressed; to them she had it all. What was there to be sad about?

"Thank you, Beth," Anna said quietly. "But it's true." She said in a tone that left no room for argument so Beth didn't push back.

"I'm terrible at communication; I do more listening than talking. This seems like a nice thing now, until I'm in a relationship with you." She cut Beth a look.

Beth flushed, imagining herself in a relationship with Anna. Anna who'd made Beth feel more heard than anyone else ever had. Listening wouldn't be so bad but she didn't say that.

"You ask about my day and I give you one worded answers; not because I'm cross but because there's nothing to tell, I don't particularly enjoy small talk so why would I come home at the end of the day to talk about the tossers at work whom I don't give a damn about?" Something told Beth that this was as close to heated as Anna got. She still sounded calm but there was a slight intensity to her voice. Beth wondered if it was a lawyer thing or an Anna thing.

"After a while, the novelty of having someone listen to your ever word wears off pretty quick. It's a lot less bearable in a long distance relationship, or at least my ex girlfriend told me so." Anna didn't sound bitter or hurt, just accepting. "And believe me, she tried to 'coax' me out of my shell."

Beth didn't think Anna was hiding in any shell.

"But this is who I am. And you can't change that." Anna cast Beth a meaningful look and Beth got the sense that they weren't talking about Anna's old relationship anymore. "You can't condition people. If they aren't willing to change, if they can't change, then maybe they aren't right for you."

Elizabeth Granger was one stubborn daughter of a gun. Anna was both impressed and slightly exasperated by it. If only Beth would apply it where it actually counted. But no, she was hell bent on beating a dead horse, thinking up tactics that would make Carrie see reason. It seemed to Anna that the only person refusing to see reason was Beth.

Anna immediately felt bad the moment that the thought occurred to her. Beth was in an emotionally abusive relationship even though she might not know it and Anna couldn't stand to the side and do nothing to help. She might try to deny it but she already cared for Beth and felt some strange form of responsibility towards the situation. She had to help and even though it was the last thing that she might do, she was going to save Beth from Carrie and from her own self.

***

Smoke curled lazily in Carrie's face. She batted it away with her hand and took another puff of the cigarette. A few feet away, Tiff was rummaging through the fridge, searching for god knew what. Thank goodness Carrie was only over at Tiff's place for sex and good company because she'd starve to death if she wanted Tiff to feed her.

Tiff always claimed to forget to buy groceries even though there was always alcohol in the fridge; the occasional wine that Carrie would bring over and beer but nothing to eat. Tiff finally gave up on her search and closed the door of the fridge with a too loud bang.

"Oops," She said with a giggle. She was a little pissed from the almost empty bottle of wine sitting on the floor with Carrie. "I'm starving." She declared. "Aren't you hungry, Carrie?"

As if on cue, Carrie's own stomach rumbled. She'd eaten the sandwich that Beth got her from the service station but the last time she'd eaten before then was almost a day ago. That was what usually happened when she was out with Tiff, they usually went to the clubs and they'd drink plenty on an empty stomach. Carrie would often forget to eat.

At least it keeps me in shape, she thought while sucking in her already flat stomach. Realising that Tiff was waiting for an answer, she looked up and said, "Sure, I'm craving food."

"Let's order takeaway." Tiff suggested. "You're paying."

Carrie smirked. Beth paid a sort of allowance to Carrie monthly for the past few months, ever since Carrie played the starving artist front drama. It was too easy to make Beth feel guilty about being wealthy and it was a game that Carrie liked to play. Either way, it was a win for Carrie – Beth would grow a spine someday and start to be assertive or she'd just continue to give Carrie more money.

"You're always leeching off me." Carrie mocked.

Tiff rolled her eyes. "And you're always leeching off your girlfriend. It's the fucking cycle of life."

"Circle." Carrie corrected, ignoring Tiff's jab. She wasn't leeching off Beth; she'd never forced Beth to give her money, in fact, she hated spending Beth's money, hated that Beth could give it all away without blinking because money had never been a problem for her.

"Whatever, I'm ordering Chinese." Tiff answered, already walking away to get her phone.

"Your ass is going to get so fat." Carrie called after her.

"More for you to grab, darling," Tiff threw over her shoulder without looking at Carrie.

Carrie huffed a laugh to herself. She took another drag of her cigarette before grinding it on the ashtray beside her. She grabbed the bottle in front of her and gulped the last drink. She couldn't help her mind drifting, trying to imagine what Beth was saying. Was she still sulking in the backseat, crying?

A slow smile spread on Carrie's smile at the thought. She quite liked the imagery; Carrie would be the last person to deny that she didn't like the effect that she had on Beth, how she became a pathetic mess when Carrie refused to bend to her will. Surely Beth must know that Carrie wasn't moved by her tears. Carrie would bend to nice gifts though. She was still smiling when Tiff returned.

"What are you smiling about, psychopath?" She asked as she settled herself on the floor besides Carrie, legs crossed over the other yoga style.

Carrie gave a coy shrug. "It's Beth, you should have seen the way she broke down when I told her I was leaving. You'd think I was serving her divorce papers."

Tiff threw her head back and laughed. "I can't believe she's that pathetic." Tiff added as she tapped away at her phone. "Food is going to be here in fifteen."

She put her phone away and leaned forward, resting her face in her palms. "You know, I reckon she'll become obsessed with you. When you break up with her, she'll send you notes and extravagant gifts." The way Tiff's eyes glittered with glee gave Carrie pause. She'd known that Tiff didn't particularly like Beth, it wasn't so much a typical envy issue. Tiff wasn't jealous that she had to share Carrie's time with Beth; Tiff was jealous that she wasn't Beth. Rich and privileged and having nothing to worry about. She didn't just envy Beth, with every single story that Carrie told her, she hated Beth.

"You're going to break up with her, aren't you?"

Carrie snorted, she had no desire to be with Beth for the rest of her life. Eventually, she might end their relationship but for now, it wasn't so much of a burden that she couldn't get away if she wanted to.

"Who knows?" Carrie asked with a mysterious smile on her lips.

Tiff narrowed her kohl lined eyes. "She is fun to keep around."

Carrie snickered, "That is one way to put it." Beth's life did provide entertainment.

"She almost got on her knees to beg me to stay." Carrie added, knowing that Tiff got a kick out of Beth's theatrics the way that she did too.

"So she's seeing the house today." Tiff said. Carrie bobbed her head in answer.

"You better hope that she doesn't fall in love with the place; next she'll be going on her knees to ask you to marry her and raise three bratty children together."

Carrie pretended to gag. "I'd fake my own death and get the hell away." She shot Tiff a coy smile. "Maybe by then, I'd have enough money to buy one of those little beach houses in Miami."

Tiff cackled. "Take me with you."

CHAPTER *NINE*

"We can't wake Simon up." Susan announced.

Immediately, the murmurs of outrage arose.

"Surely there's something that we could do," Nancy said, wearing a frown on her face and her hands on her belly. Her husband, Hunter was standing behind her, his hands on her shoulder. "Keep him away from the visitors." Her voice soured on the word visitors. The word could be easily exchanged for intruders and it would still fit in nicely.

"They'll want a tour." Felicity warned as if Susan didn't already know it. Moving Simon was out of the question, the environment he was in was supposed to be stable, it had been created that way to make sure that Simon's psychedelic trip was easy – if it was tampered with, then he might not return the same way that he'd been mentally.

But Susan didn't need to tell them that, they all knew the implications of waking Simon up or moving him.

"Maybe we should be talking to a lawyer, surely these people can't just walk in and demand the house. We've covered rent for months ahead." Hunter said furiously.

It wasn't a bad suggestion, they were clearly out of their depths legal wise. Susan gave Hunter a half smile.

"I'll speak to a friend who is a lawyer."

"Do you think?..." Nancy began before pausing as if she couldn't bear to ask the question in full.

"Think what?" Felicity asked sharply.

"What if they're coming over because the new landlady wants the house?" Nancy finally asked.

Felicity didn't have much patience for that. She rolled her eyes and scoffed. "They can't do that." She said in a voice that was supposed to sound confident but came out hesitant, a little questioning. She looked to Hunter for reassurance but his own doubt was shining in his eyes.

"They can't kick us out." Susan said firmly. That much she knew, but something told her that this wasn't a friendly visit either. "And we'll keep them away from Simon. Make up an excuse about how he's sick and has been isolated."

Felicity and Nancy shared another look. "What if they call to report instead?"

Susan felt the onset of an headache, she rubbed several fingers on her temple and sighed. "Let's not get ahead of ourselves yet. I'll speak to my lawyer friend for legal advice. In the meantime, I would appeal to all of you to keep calm. Clear everything that could possibly be suspicious."

They hung on to her every word, nodding when they needed to.

"There's no need to act like anything's going on. Let's just go about our daily business. Do the things that you usually do today — follow the rota."

She shot them another smile, one that was supposed to convey calm and control, she'd mastered it over the years as a therapist. She saw the smile take effects on their faces, suddenly they looked more optimistic. She often found that all people needed was a course of action to follow and they would be fine.

She'd just given them purpose.

***

They were less than forty minutes away from Margate. Beth had stopped talking about ways to trick Carrie into commitment, in fact for the past ten minutes, they'd been mostly silent, not making any attempts at conversation. Anna was the last person to cheer for small talk but she found herself preferring a talkative Beth to this silent brooding womxn beside her.

Anna needed to do something, she needed to stall this trip.

"Are you nervous?" She asked.

Beth startled a little as if she'd half forgotten that Anna was with her in the car. She shook her head from side to side. It had started to get a little windy so Anna had pulled up the roof of the car. But Beth had kept her window wound down and her hair whipped around her face. It was such a cliché thing to think but Anna couldn't help but notice how young she looked. The slight bags under her eyes stood out, revealing the stare of her exhaustion. The sparkling of her eyes said otherwise though, she looked alive. Anna wanted to reach out, to capture that look on her face. She wanted to hide it in her own mind forever, to summon at will on bad days.

"No?" Anna asked, focusing on the womxn in front of her rather than the thoughts that she sparked. "Are you sure?" She wasn't sure what she was trying to do. Anna didn't want her chickening out of the trip in fright but she wouldn't mind a bit of nerves.

"What?" Beth laughed. "You're saying it like not being nervous is a bad thing."

Anna didn't say anything at first. If Beth noticed that Anna was driving slower in the past ten minutes than she'd been when their journey started out, then she didn't show it.

"You don't need to hide how you feel with me, Beth." Anna told her.

Beth's smile wavered for a second. "Is it because you're my lawyer?"

"Because we're friends." Anna corrected firmly.

This time, Beth did smile, wider. "Oh, I wasn't aware. At what moment did we transcend from a strict lawyer-client relationship to friendship?"

Usually, Anna found it difficult to tell when most people jested. Their jokes tended to fall flat but with Beth, it was different, it was clear as day when she was teasing Anna.

"The moment where you asked me for relationship advice." Anna deadpanned. "And I told you about my ex-girlfriend."

Beth threw back her head and laughed.

"Look at us, bonding over relationship woes." Beth said wryly. "I guess this is where I tell you that you're an absolute queen and your ex-girlfriend is an idiot for dumping you."

Anna barely resisted the urge to say the same thing to Beth. You're an absolute queen, Beth, this is where I tell you that your girlfriend is a fucking disgraceful and you should dump her.

That would be one perfect way to take a sledgehammer to all the progress that the two of them had made this morning. But Anna would get to say the words to Beth soon, if things went well with this trip, Carrie was going to get her miserable arse dumped.

"She didn't dump me." Anna corrected, she drove past a sign, barely catching the end of the words written on it — Area of Outstanding Natural Beauty. An idea suddenly occurred to her.

"You dumped her? You're such a heartbreaker." Beth was saying.

Anna snorted. "It's a little less dramatic than that and it was a mutual decision to end things. We're on good terms, we still text occasionally." Anna wasn't really one for theatrics and for all Lindsey's complaints about Anna being closed off, she too was practical. The last Anna had heard from her, she'd gotten engaged to some paediatrician. Anna wished her well.

"That's nice." Beth said. Anna could tell that she meant it too.

"So are you nervous?" Anna asked again.

"Yeah, a little. Carrie and I were supposed to make this journey together. There's a reason why I've been mostly uninterested about claiming this property," Beth said, taking in a deep breath. "My aunt passed it to me in her will. She died a few months ago."

Beth blinked a few times, she pretended to look outside the window but it really was a ruse to gather herself. Anna let her have that.

"We were really close, she was a nonsense womxn. She was the first womxn in my family to join in on the family business — mind you, we've been doing this stuff for about four generations now. She refused to let all her brothers handle all the business and she fought tooth and nail to be trusted. When she passed, I was devastated."

"As one should be. Your aunt sounds amazing." Anna said softly.

Beth wiped away a traitorous tear sliding down her cheek. "She was. Finding out that she left something to me wasn't the joyful moment you'd think and claiming it, checking it out felt like revisiting her death. If I pretend that it didn't exist, then maybe my aunt is still alive."

Anna understood that. Often, people thought that the five stages of grief were cut and dry. Denial onto anger onto bargaining onto depression and unto acceptance. But it wasn't exactly like that, years after her own mother had passed, she could say she'd learned to live with it a little, maybe even find acceptance. Then she'd find herself returning to the first stage again; denial. There was no way that her beloved mother was gone, that she would never see her again or hear her laugh that her quiet laugh again. Surely people didn't just die.

"I'm sorry for your loss, Beth."

Beth nodded, likely already used to hearing those words. Those inadequate words that never even soothed any part of the pain. Anna hated hearing them but they were all that she could offer.

"Thank you, Anna." That was Beth ever gracious to the end.

"If you're nervous, it's okay. I know a place we could hang out, let the time run for a while." Anna suggested.

A curious light entered Beth's eyes. "Really?"

"Kent Downs is close. We could park the car and take a break." Anna suggested with a shrug, as if to say no pressure.

"Let's go." Beth added.

Anna only had to drive a little further. The skies seemed clearer around this place; a bright blue that was stunning to look at. There were a few clouds in the sky, Anna thought that one looked like a bunny, she pointed it out to Beth who squinted observingly at it.

Although Anna had killed the engine and brought down the roof, they were still sitting in the car.

"Yeah, it does look a little like a bunny." Beth agreed slowly but it was clear that she didn't think so.

Anna rolled her eyes. "You can disagree with me, you know."

It is perfectly fine to disagree with me. You don't have to pretend just to keep the peace with me." Anna chided her gently. Beth gave a sheepish smile in return.

"Sorry, force of habit." Now, Anna didn't think that Beth was talking about just Carrie. This ran deeper than that. Perhaps her relationship with her parents. Beth had been groomed to be a pushover for a long time, it was not surprising anymore that she applied the same tactics to her own relationship.

"Let's get out of the car and see some beauty." Anna said, reaching out and giving Beth's arm a love tap. Beth raised a quick eyebrow Anna realised that this was the first time that either of them was initiating physical contact.

She waited a beat to see if Beth would rebuke her for it. There was a high chance that Anna had mistaken Beth's politeness for friendship, that was possible.

Instead, Beth opened her door and climbed out of the car. "What are you waiting for?"

Anna copied her actions. The two of them walked together, close enough that if they swung their arms, they would touch. But they walked in companionable silence.

If someone had told Anna yesterday that she would be getting along easily with her client, and that she would want to offer help above what she normally did, what her job specified, then Anna would have laughed as if it was a big lie.

Here she was though, doing the exact opposite. It was nice though.

"It's so stunning out here. I don't think I've ever been anywhere like this place in my whole life." Beth said, breaking the silence between them.

Anna resurfaced from her thoughts, she drank in the sight like Beth did; clear skies, lush grass covering the ground they walked and shrubs of different kinds of flowers before them, and from the looks of it, extending a long distance. Anna didn't believe in the existence of any God or even in paradise. She'd never been able to understand those people who had tried to comfort her by telling her that her mother was in a better place. There was no better place after death, there was just oblivion and nothingness. But for the first time, Anna tried to imagine a paradise after death, if this was how it looked like, then it wasn't at all a bad place to go to after one died.

"Me neither." Anna said. "I mean, I've heard of about it a while ago but I've never been interested in visiting."

"We've been missing out." Beth said with a wry smile.

Anna exhaled a tiny sigh of relief, she was glad that Beth liked this place. It was tranquil, definitely a place to go for peace of mind from all the crap of the world.

"I don't know much about AONBs, could you tell me about how they come to be?" Beth asked, she laughed a little. "Actually, I don't know anything except that I see them on online maps."

Anna didn't know why Beth thought that she would know either but she couldn't deny that she liked the way that Beth looked at her, as if she was smarter than anyone else that she knew. She was however not very knowledgeable on nature. "I don't know much either, but I do know that the government set up environmental organisations to help preserve the last bits of nature. So there's probably an authority in charge of this place, to make sure that the environment stays the same way; free from pollution."

Beth nodded as if Anna had given a rousing speech on climate change. "That makes sense." She was still glancing around the vast open field, eyes as wide as saucers as she took in everything.

I want her to look at me like that, Anna thought. She must be going mad, where did that thought come from?

"I wonder what kinds of animals make their home here." Beth said.

"Maybe the tamer ones," Anna said unsurely.

"Likely, I don't see many trees around," Beth agreed. "Maybe they let cows graze here sometimes."

Anna could see that happening.

They continued walking with Beth pointing out the names of plants, she'd tell Anna their botanical names and also the common names that they were known by. Normally, it wasn't information that Anna usually cared about but Beth made everything sound interesting. She didn't just rattle facts off the top of her head, she made Anna curious to learn.

Anna was about to ask questions on a blue flower when Beth sighed. Anna tensed up, knowing that she was about to start talking about Carrie again.

"I wish Carrie would have come, she might have loved to see this." Beth said.

Anna couldn't imagine snotty Carrie stopping to smell the roses. Carrie must not like to look at things that made her feel less beautiful, it was clear as day that all she cared about was herself.

Anna made a noncommittal hum as response to Beth. "Oh, look, is that a rabbit?" Anna pointed at nothing. Beth frowned and looked around, following Anna's finger.

"Where?" She asked.

"Oh, it's gotten away." Anna answered, waving a hand carelessly as if it didn't matter. She expected that Beth would launch into some educative fun facts about rabbits.

"You keep telling me not to worry about her, that this is merely a blip that will pass."

It had to be a cosmic joke; because there was no way that Beth had misinterpreted Anna's words this bad. This isn't a blip! Anna wanted to shout. Your relationship is toxic and you need to end it before you lose yourself completely. Alas, she couldn't say that either, not yet.

Anna gritted her teeth and swallowed yet another set of Carrie insults.

"Carrie sometimes doesn't know what is good for her until you slap it in her face. That's what I need to do, slap her in the face with this, make her listen and truly understand." Beth was saying passionately. Anna was only half listening. Perhaps nature wasn't such a good idea after all. It was time to switch tactics.

"I have to pee." Anna announced suddenly, cutting Beth off mid Carrie spiel.

Beth blinked a few times, "Here?"

Despite herself, Anna threw back her head and laughed hard, she was still giggling when she answered. "Of course not, silly."

"We have to leave here and find a service station. I'm sure you're hungry too, we could grab a bite to eat."

As if on cue, Beth's stomach grumbled aloud and Anna smiled.

"I am hungry." Beth said sheepishly. Anna wanted to ask her when last she'd eaten but she was afraid that the answer would be Carrie related. It seemed that there wasn't a topic on earth that was Carrie safe. Which was why Beth needed to eat, if her mouth was stuffed then she wouldn't talk about Carrie.

Anna laughed at her own thoughts, imagining a Beth with her mouth stuffed full of food. Beth was too polite and well mannered to talk with her mouth full, yes, that would be the perfect solution.

"What's funny?" Beth asked with a puzzled look on her face. Anna shook her head. "No reason."

***

This service station looked a lot better than the last one that they'd encountered. Anna parked her car besides a rougher looking car; the paint was chipped off and the vehicle looked like it was one more start from breaking down completely. She exchanged a look with Beth and knew that she was thinking the same thing. They headed into the service station, pleasantly surprised to find it well stocked. There were several vending machine for different kinds of snacks. Again, Beth's stomach rumbled.

She shook her head. "Sorry, I haven't eaten since yesterday afternoon."

Anna sensed that there was a story behind that answer but she didn't ask. "Well, let's get some food in your stomach. My treat."

Beth scoffed. "No way, I'm not letting you pay."

Anna raised her brow. "We lawyers can't compare to landowner money but we still make enough for ourselves; enough to treat our friends to lunch. I reckon I'll even have some change to spare for lunch."

Beth flushed guiltily. "Sorry. I didn't mean to imply." Once again, Anna found herself silently cursing Carrie's name to hell and beyond. If there was a place worse than hell, it was still too good for the likes of Carrie.

"Beth, I'm kidding." Anna told her, she patted her shoulder gently. Ever since she'd touched her in the car, Anna had quickly realised that she wanted to do it again. She wanted to hold her hand and to brush hair away from her face.

"Oh, sorry." Beth said tightly. Anna sighed.

"Please don't apologise. We're friends, remember? Friends don't get mad at each other for trivial things." Anna told her firmly. She suspected that like her, Beth didn't have too many friends either. Maybe it was a Carrie thing, maybe Beth didn't like socialising.

"So, can I buy you lunch?" Anna asked.

Beth flushed and before she could give a verbal answer, someone burst in through the doors and almost ran right into Beth.

"Shit, I'm sorry." A teenage boy apologised effusively. He had a head full of dishevelled curly hair and was wearing a red shirt with a name tag on it that read; Clyde, cashier.

"It's no worry." Beth said, her words breaking from completion when he brushed past them.

He dashed past them and nearly collided with an older man wearing a similar shirt, Anna spied his own name tag and realised that he was the manager of the service station.

"Late again, Clyde. This is the fifth time this month." The manager sneered at him. He was a thin, reedy man with a receding hairline. Anna thought that he kind of looked like Alan Sugar. If Alan Sugar had buck teeth and big ears.

"He kind of looks like Alan Sugar." Anna whispered close to Beth's ear.

Beth muffled her laugh against her palm, trapping it before it would escape and alert the manager to their presence. He might not be so rude to them since they were customers and Anna would find the change comical, how he'd force a smile on his face to save his dignity. She had met people like him, bullies keeping up the ruse of being pleasant but unleashing their frustration on innocent people when they were alone. Yes, the boy might have been late but it didn't give the manager the right to shout at him like he was a toddler. Even if he was a toddler, shouting at him wasn't acceptable either.

"You sleep in that shitty car of yours just outside this place and you still can't wake up early to open this place." The manager was saying, from where Anna stood, she saw spittle flying from his mouth and landing on Clyde's face.

"He's awful." Beth said.

Anna nodded her head in agreement.

"I'm sorry, I overslept." Clyde's back was turned to Anna and Beth but he sounded pretty close to tears.

The manager jabbed a finger in Clyde's face. "That isn't an excuse. You're fired."

Clyde was definitely crying now. "Please don't fire me, I swear it'll never happen again. I need this job."

"Actually, you can't just fire him." Anna said suddenly.

Both men turned around to stare at her.

"And who are you?" The manager asked with a sour look on his face.

"I'm a lawyer." Anna announced. She'd been telling the truth when she told Beth that she didn't feel much passion for law. It had been a practical decision that she'd made. But for the first time, Anna felt something like pride announcing who she was and what she did.

The manager's eyes fixed on her, he had no doubt taken in her formal clothes and deduced that she was telling the truth.

"I can fire whoever I want to. He's my employee to do with as I deem fit." He snapped.

Anna kept a pleasant smile on her face.

"Not according to recent law, you can't. Not especially since there are two witnesses in front of you who witnessed you belittle and emotionally abuse your employee. Mr. Clyde can sue for hundreds of thousands and a decent court would order you to pay." Anna explained curtly, enjoying the way the manager's face blanched in fear. The mention of a huge sum of money had done that.

"Clyde, how do you get paid? Is it an hourly wage or monthly?" Anna asked, she kept her tone neutral, as if they were having a conversation about the weather and not a possible lawsuit. Clyde was looking at her as if she was an avenging angel. As if he couldn't quite believe his eyes. "Um, it's a monthly wage." He stammered. "And I do get a staff discount." He added.

Anna nodded sagely, her hands in her pocket. She was enjoying herself, putting fright into this man.

"If you fire him, you need to pay him for this month."
The manager, seething, opened his mouth to argue but Anna raised up a hand. "I'm not finished."

"And yes, you have to pay. It's the law, Mr. Manager." She said sweetly.

"Plus the lawsuit." Beth added. Anna had half forgotten that Beth was besides her. Beth sent Anna a conspiratorial wink.

"What's it going to be?" Anna asked.

"Go back to your post, you idiot." The manager expostulated.

Anna took a step forward. "You can't talk to your staff like that." She warned the manager darkly and gave her business card to Clyde. "Call me when you need."

He flinched and waved Clyde away. Clyde scurried away, shooting Anna looks of gratefulness. The manager walked away, steps hastened as if Anna would remind him of another point against him.

"That was something." Beth said the moment the manager was out of sight.

She was practically bouncing on the balls of her feet and looking at Anna as if she'd handed her the keys of the world.

"You're amazing. The way you swooped in to defend that kid." Beth said, she assumed Anna's stance and stern look. "I thought that guy was going to pee his trouser."

"It was nothing." Anna said, unsure why she was feeling a little shy under Beth's gaze. "I did what I was supposed to do, I would have done it for anyone else." It wasn't exactly the truth. Of all the areas she could have specialised in, Anna had chosen one of the most impersonal ones. She could have become a criminal defence solicitor but she chose not to be. Even though she wasn't a bad person, she wasn't exactly the nicest either. The old Anna would have walked into this place and ignored the row between the manager and his employee. But the new Anna, the one that knew Beth wanted to make a difference in any way that she could.

"Still." Beth said.

The two of them continued to smile at each other until Clyde returned. It was only then that she realised the proximity. She was standing so close to Beth, enough to see the dotted freckles on her cheeks.

"Ma'am, I want to thank you for helping me out there." Clyde said shyly.

"It's Anna."

"Thank you, Anna. I really need this job," Clyde said. "I think you two should try your luck at the slot machine." He gave them a small wink.

Beth and Anna exchanged looks.

"I've got a fiver." Anna said.

"If you win a million pounds, we're sharing it equally." Beth teased.

"If I win a million pounds, I'm quitting my job forever and going on endless vacation." Anna said.

The two of them walked to the slot machine near the cashier's counter. "What would you do if you won half a million pounds?"

Beth was rich, yes, she owned several properties but she didn't think that she had that much in cash in her bank account.

"I don't know." Beth gave a shrug. "I'm comfortable. There's nothing I think of — and this is not me bragging about being rich. I don't want too many things, I'm content with my home, the food I have and I don't have use for a car."

"I'm not sure if I'm making much sense." Beth added self consciously.

"I understand you perfectly. You're saying that you're content with having little, that you don't wish for more." Anna explained.

Beth nodded. "I feel like all money has ever done for me is bring problems. I know that I'm privileged and that many people have it much worse. But if my family was ordinary, I'd be able to do whatever the hell I like, there wouldn't be this pressure to expand the family wealth without a care for what I want to do."

Anna nodded to let her know that she was paying attention as she rummaged through her purse.

"And with Carrie, she's always been insecure about the difference in our social status. I've tried to level it several times but it's all that she can see." Beth continued, a note of frustration creeping into her voice. It was perhaps the first time that she was talking about her girlfriend with frustration. It was a good thing. It was high time that she realised that Carrie was being deliberately difficult.

"I found a fiver." Anna announced, taking out a five pound note.

Beth smiled distractedly. Anna slotted the note into the machine and waited.

They remained in companionable silence for a few seconds. Beth wore a slight frown on her face as if she was still thinking about Carrie.

The screen of the slot machine rolled out a message. Anna punched a fist in the air.

"Forty six pounds!" She cheered. A smile broke out on Beth's face as Anna did a little dance in celebration.

"We're rich, we'll never have to buy a single thing in our lives anymore." Beth drawled sarcastically.

"That's the spirit, Granger."

"Total coincidence that you saved Clyde's job and happened to win forty six pounds the next minute." Beth said, deadpan.

Anna wore a look of mock seriousness on her face. "You know what they say, it pays to have someone on the inside rooting for you."

Beth smiled and broke free at last. "You're something else, Fenwick."

"Something good, I hope." Anna said.

Beth shook her head. "Your ex-girlfriend is a cow."

The smile on Anna's face dimmed. Not that it was a sore subject to discuss her ex girlfriend but it was a little uncomfortable because she'd been right. Just because Anna was open now to Beth didn't mean that she would continue to be.

It was Anna's nature to be closed off. Even now, it was Beth who did all the talking. Anna only contributed when it was necessary.

"Too much?" Beth asked, noticing Anna's silence.

"Let's just not talk about relationships, present or past." Anna suggested with a half smile.

Beth nodded quickly. "We have a deal."

"Good. Let's go cash out our earnings. I'm going to buy you lunch, Madam."

Beth pretended to swoon. "You certainly know the way to a womxn's heart."

Anna was smiling but inside, she wondered if Beth was flirting with her or if she even knew herself.

"What about the tenants?" Beth asked, a worried light entering her eyes. "We've already delayed them enough."

The strangest thing was that Anna had already forgotten about the specifics of their trip. This wasn't a situation of two friends hanging out. She'd let herself get carried away by Beth. She wasn't sure if that was a good thing or not.

"Don't worry, you're the landlady, Beth and anyway, I will call them and let them know that we might be late."

"Wouldn't that give the wrong impression?" Beth asked worriedly.

Anna touched a comforting hand on her shoulder before she realised what she was doing. She removed her hand as subtly as she could. Beth wasn't stupid; she was bound to realise that Anna was touching her on purpose. Anna almost winced as she imagined Beth getting the wrong message and trying to let her down gently, reminding her that she had a girlfriend that she loved and was devoted to. Anna already had a few embarrassing things to happen to her but this would no doubt be the most embarrassing one.

"It's fine, Beth. You're the landlady."

"I know but I still have a few principles that I like to follow."

"I'll speak to the tenants and let them know that we'll be coming in a little later. Don't worry about it." Anna said to reassure Beth.

She took out her phone and dialled the number. The phone was answered on the second ring, as if Dr. Parker had been sitting by the phone and waiting for them to call.

"Anna Fenwick, solicitor." Anna said into the phone.

***

Susan gripped the phone harder.

"Yes, that's perfectly fine." Susan said. "Of course, we will."

She muttered a noncommittal goodbye before realising that Anna Fenwick had hung up already.

"Well, what did she say?" Felicity asked.

Of all of them, she might be the one on edge the most. Simon was her husband. Susan plastered a smile on her face that likely didn't look half convincing.

"She said that they will be late but didn't offer an explanation. Sounded quite stern." Susan frowned. Whoever Anna Fenwick was, Susan didn't like her.

"They're definitely going to call the police on us if they find out." Nancy moaned.

"Let's not get ahead of ourselves here!" Susan snapped, suddenly furious at how easily they all panicked. Surely she'd taught them better than that.

"Have you got in touch with your friend?" Hunter asked.

Susan brushed back her bangs from her face, they were starting to grow a little too long that they now covered past her face. "I left a message. But he's yet to get back to me."

Nancy who sat down on the sofa looked up from where she'd been frantically tapping away on her screen. "I've been googling our rights. It says here that we cannot be kicked out without a notice and that the lawyer will try to push for us to settle outside of court — that is if they're trying to gain possession of this place."

Everybody blinked at Nancy, no doubt ashamed that it was the pregnant womxn amongst them that was actually looking for reasonable solutions instead of panicking like the rest of them were.

"Well done, Nancy." Susan gave her an approving nod. "We've made sure to hide anything suspicious. This delay buys us enough time to cover all our bases."

"All we can do now is wait for them to arrive."

***

Anna and Beth found themselves in a family owned restaurant that clearly worshipped the British Monarchy. There was a cut out cardboard of Princess Diana as the centrepiece on the wall behind the counter. There was a signed autograph of Princess Sophie framed on the wall above their booth.

The food was good and the wine was cheap. Anna was on her second drink, sloshing the leftover liquid in her cup like a wine taster.

She knew that if she glanced at the mirror, her face would be flushed a deep red and she would be smiling wide. She hadn't stopped smiling since they stepped foot in the restaurant. Anna couldn't remember the last time she'd been so relaxed.
She'd never felt so at ease with anybody, not until she met Beth.

"I can't believe I've never taken an impromptu road trip before, it's definitely nice to stop and smell the roses once a while." Anna said as she downed the rest of her wine. She saw that Beth was looking at her a little wearily so she waved her hand. "I can handle my alcohol." She said.

"Your voice is slurring a little, you're obviously a lightweight." Beth said, she looked a little amused staring at Anna.

Anna waved again. "I'm fine. Yes, it's true, I don't drink often. Maybe I should, maybe tolerance levels for alcohol is increased through continual practice."

"Continual practice like being an alcoholic?" Beth asked in amusement.

Anna applauded slowly. "Exactly, you just get me, Beth."

Beth looked taken aback by Anna's words but she smiled. "I'm glad." She was polishing off the last of her chocolate cake. She raised her fork in a toast. "To you, Anna. Else my stomach would still be growling up a storm."

"Twenty questions," Beth announced before taking a bite of her cake. "Let's play twenty questions."

"This is that game where we both take turns asking each other questions, right?" Anna asked. They were the only customers in the restaurant, save aside a womxn sitting at a far booth on the other side of the room near the window. For a moment, Anna wondered if she was waiting for someone; a friend perhaps or a romantic partner. For some reason, Anna found herself remembering sitting at lunch alone in high school, she hadn't exactly been bullied by her peers then. She was smart enough to be beloved by teachers, that gave her an edge over her classmates. They had hated her but apart from the usual taunts and snide remarks, they didn't bother touching her.

Anna also saw Beth in that womxn, in the way she kept glancing expectantly at the door. The way Beth still held out hope about Carrie, that perhaps she would come to her senses.

"Yeah, that's the one." Beth said.

"Sure, go ahead and ask." Anna said.

"Favourite colour?" Beth asked.

Anna paused, surprised by the mundane question. She'd expected the hard hitting stuff, wasn't that the point of the game? To discover the other person's deepest desires and darkest secrets. Then again, how would she know? She'd never played the game before.

Beth laughed at the puzzled look on Anna's face. "You look so surprised."

"I expected you to ask me to tell you all my deepest darkest secrets." Anna said truthfully, flushing when Beth laughed.

"I already know your deepest darkest secret." Beth said dismissively. "We've been talking about heavy stuff all morning. That stuff is important to know about someone but the little questions also matter."

"I don't have a favourite colour." Anna said. "I have a preference for muted colours though. They suit me better." But she was beginning to like blue, clear sky blue that reminded her of a certain somebody's eyes.

Beth seemed to appraise Anna's style, noting her cream coloured blouse and maroon jacket. "Yeah, they suit you."

Anna toyed with the rim of her glass. "And what is your favourite colour?" She asked.

Beth smiled. "Green."

"Why?" Anna asked. She was pretty sure that she was breaking the rules of the game. They were supposed to take turns asking each other questions. Beth didn't seem to mind though.

"I associate it with health and nature." Beth said unabashedly. "What do you do on your days off from work?"

Anna smiled ruefully. "You're assuming that I get days off from work."

Beth gasped in outrage. "Why not?"

"I rarely take them. I like working." Anna said, before today she might have been fooled by the conviction in her tone but not today, she liked her job, sure but the reason she rarely took days off was because she didn't have anyone to spend it with. Her mom lived too far that Anna visit her all the time and she'd refused when Anna asked her to come live with her. Her mother claimed to like the quaint town that Anna had grown up in.

Beth narrowed her eyes. "You're lying."

"Fine, I'm lying. I don't really have much of a life outside of work." It didn't sound pathetic for Anna to finally admit it. Maybe because she knew that Beth wouldn't judge her for it.

"So, go out there and create a life. Go dancing, partying or whatever extroverts like to do for fun." Beth said, taking a sip of the water in front of her. Anna shrugged. "Aren't those things that you do with friends and not alone?"

"How are you going to get any friends if you don't go out there and make them?" Beth asked.

Anna didn't want to get into the specifics of her life, it was exhausting enough thinking about it. "Alright. What do you do for fun, Beth?"

"I stay at home, take care of my plants and watch TV. I'm introverted, people don't really do it for me. Besides, when I was abroad for university, I did all the wild things I could think of − kind of like a bucket list. I partied hard, smoked, dyed my hair purple and got into flings."

Anna tried and failed to imagine that kind of Beth, living her best life because there would be none of that when she returned home.

"It was fun, sure." She shrugged. "And now, I spend the rest of my days recovering from my wildest days. I do go out with my cousins when they're around and occasionally accompany Carrie to these gallery openings with all sort of artists attending."

There was a pause between them. Anna waved over the waiter to pay and she was handed the receipt.

"Let's go." Anna said, she stood up and swayed a little. "Wow, I think I drank a little too much."

Beth came to stand near her as she took her first steps, to make sure that she didn't fall.

Anna smiled. "You're too kind."

A worried frown made its way on Beth's face. "I don't think it's safe for you to drive."

"I agree. Can you drive?'

Beth blushed and turned her head away. "I do have license but I haven't driven in forever."

"That isn't a problem, I'll guide you."

CHAPTER *TEN*

I'll guide you. Famous last words. Beth had been pretty damned perfect to Anna but she was indeed a terrible driver.

"Go slow!" Anna told Beth as she took a fast turn on a particularly twisty road. Beth hit the break and the car came to a sudden halt, sending Anna almost face first into the dashboard, she caught herself barely in time thanks to the seat belt around her. She'd put it on five minutes into Beth's driving.

The coffee cup on the dashboard swayed and fell into Beth's lap, the contents of it sloshing into Beth's lap and soaking her skirt.

"Damn it." Beth swore.

"Damn is right, you're an awful driver and you're going to drive us straight to hell." Anna exclaimed. Beth shot her a look that was a little annoyed.

"If you hadn't drunk so much, maybe we wouldn't be in this situation." She snapped back.

"How ever did you pass your test?" Anna asked. "Maybe your driving instructor got sick of being near death every time you drove so he just passed you."

"Ha ha, you're so clever." Beth sassed.

Anna reached forward to take the now empty cup, she set it in the cup holder where it should have been in the first place. They'd gotten the coffee from a convenience store alongside several breath analyzers. The coffee hadn't sobered Anna enough for her to drive and the breath analyzers told the both of them what they already knew; that Anna had drunk enough to make her unfit to drive.

"I need new clothes." Beth moaned.

"Eyes on the road, princess," Anna reminded her. "You're going to have to make a turn in the new minute, if I remember correctly."

"Good on you for getting a car with no GPS." Beth said sarcastically.
"It's a vintage car, I wouldn't expect you to understand, princess," Anna quipped. She oddly enjoyed sparring with Beth. It was kind of attractive.

"Princess?" Beth said, she took her eyes off the road to glare at Anna. "Where did that come from?"

"It just came to me naturally." Anna said easily.

"I'll show you who's the princess." Beth said.

"Beth Granger, eyes on the road!" Anna warned just as Beth drove past the turn she was supposed to make.

"For the love of life, Beth." Anna said with a mix of horror and fascination, how could one person be so terrible at driving?

"I'm sorry, okay." She sounded a little close to tears as she hit the break again and the car came to a screeching halt. This time, Anna had braced herself and didn't go face first into the dashboard.

"Thank you for not killing us." Anna said cheerfully.

Beth scoffed a watery laugh, "You're welcome." She glanced around and saw that they were in the countryside, the road stretched ahead and there was nothing in sight; no businesses or constructions.

"What do we do now?" She asked.

Anna took out her phone and checked. "There's no bloody reception."

It was early afternoon now, the sun beating down on them.

"Nothing on my phone either, plus it's almost flat."

Anna squinted in the distance. "If I'm correct then we're somewhere close to Canterbury. I once read on the news that the Unvaredonia Community has their abode somewhere around here."

Beth cast her a look. "What's the Unvaredonia Community?"

"Ever heard of Amish people?" Anna asked. "The Unvaredonia are kind of like that; religious people who have secluded themselves from society and given up all personal possessions to live together."

"And what makes you think it's a good idea to head into the midst of those kind of people?" Beth asked with such outrage in her voice that Anna almost giggled.

"You're acting like I told you that we're going to join them." Anna mocked. "We're just going to ask for directions and a change of clothes. Don't you want to get out of this skirt?"

She sensed Beth's stance wavering. In the end, Beth sighed. "I'm wary of religious people, Anna. Plus we're two queer womxns, I don't think they want that sort of thing in their community."

Anna frowned, she hadn't thought of it that way. "I understand your concerns, Beth but the worst they can do it throw us out. It's a free country."

"Alright, I trust you." Beth said casually, not understanding that those words meant a lot to Anna.

"It's time for you to get behind the wheel again and please, for the love of all things holy, just listen to my navigations." Anna stressed. Beth smirked.

"I make no promises." She said cheekily.
Anna made a sign of the cross as Beth started the car.

***

Beth was feeling pretty proud of herself when she took the windy bend that led them right into the Unvaredonia Community. There were only a few buildings, strange little houses with picket fences surround them. There was a clothes shop on the right side of the road and after that a shop that had no sign in front of it. Beth was still wary about the place but Anna looked calm enough. When Beth parked the car, they came out and headed towards the clothes shop.

There were very few people out on the street; there was an old lady wearing the strangest garb and watering the garden in front of her house and two men walking somewhere. Beth felt their eyes on them, no doubt the two of them stuck out like sore thumbs.

They walked into the store and Beth was hit with the smell of old clothes and some other musty smell that she couldn't identify. The shop was smaller on the inside, with only a few racks of clothes that Beth didn't even want to be caught dead in.

There was an older womxn sitting on a chair and reading a tattered book. Beth exchanged looks with Anna.

You approach her, it was your idea to come here in the first place, Beth was saying with her eyes.

And you're the one that got us lost with your terrible driving, Anna shot back silently.

Beth threw exasperated hands up and marched over to the womxn. "Good afternoon, ma'am. Sorry to bother you but my friends and I are lost, we were on the way to Margate when we missed our turn."

The womxn looked up and Beth was surprised that she wasn't that old; maybe in her early forties, her hair was long and packed in an intricate up-do that was actually kind of pretty. It was the clothes that she was wearing however that looked ridiculous and ugly; to Beth there was no difference between this frumpy looking boxy shaped gown and wearing an actual sack. It didn't help that the gown was an ugly shade of beige. Beth struggled to hold on to her already strained smile. They hadn't been here up to ten minutes and Beth already thought that it was the worst place on earth.

"Hello, dear." The womxn said as if she hadn't registered a word that Beth had said. She stood up and her eyes immediately fixed on the dark blot on the front of her skirt.

"You need a change of clothes." The womxn said and began to walk towards the clothing racks. At least she wasn't totally hard of hearing. Beth would be taking any wins at this point. If she was superstitious, she might have said that their trip was cursed; first Carrie had refused to go with them then they'd taken a detour and were no doubt going to arrive late to the house in Margate. One fucking problem after the other.

It wasn't so bad though, Beth had gotten to know Anna. She was a little afraid to admit to herself that apart from all, today might be the best day of her life. She hadn't had this much fun since... she was born. Even admitting it to herself made her feel a little guilty. You have a girlfriend, get yourself together, she told herself.

"Is that womxn deaf?" Anna whispered in Beth's ear. Her lips brushing the shell of her ear and it took everything in Beth not to shiver. What was wrong with her?

"She literally ignored everything you said and focused on what she wanted." Anna said in that same low tone.

"Last chance to run away from here." Beth said, only half joking.

"Here you go," the womxn suddenly appeared before them. Anna startled and jumped nearly two feet in the air. Beth barely held back her laughter; laughter that sound turned to horror when she saw the garment that the womxn was holding in her hand.

"No way," She breathed out and then muttered a hurried apology, "I mean, it's…"

"It's something, we're thankful." Anna cut in smoothly.

"How much would it be?" Beth said. She didn't want to buy this hideous floral skirt, it seemed to be made of the same material as this womxn's gown, a scratchy cotton material that made a crackling sound when Beth rubbed it between her fingers. She would develop a skin rash wearing this. And would it even fit her? Beth had always loved her curves, she had generous hips that made her look good in almost anything but she doubted that she would be able to pull this off.

"It's nothing, go on, try it in the back." The womxn said with a small kind smile. Beth felt a little guilty about hating the skirt, especially since she was being given it for free.

She sent Anna a questioning look. Anna gave a small nod and Beth wandered to the back of the store. There was a small fitting room, she swiped the curtain to the side and stepped into it. She slid the curtain back and stripped from her ruined skirt. There was surprisingly no mirror inside the changing room and Beth wondered why.

Maybe it was a religious thing. She wore the new skirt and wasn't surprised when the baggy material fell limply on her, making any curves that she might have had nonexistent.

She returned back to where Anna and the womxn were conversing. To Anna's credit, she hid her horror well, only glancing at Beth's skirt for a brief moment before looking away.

"Hey Beth, Elder Hannah was just inviting us to stay for dinner but I told her about the urgency of thing we have." Anna said with a tight smile. Beth was baffled at the title but she would ask Anna that later. She was more focused on the pending problem; this strange womxn was inviting them to have dinner. If they didn't wear normal clothes, what if they didn't eat normal food either? Plus isn't it so early for dinner?

"We are kind of in a hurry, Elder Hannah." Beth said, trying to mimic Anna's apologetic tone.

Elder Hannah shook her head. "The community is aware of your presence, we don't get visitors very often." Oh, no, how could that be? Beth thought caustically.

"It would be very impolite to let you go without offering you the Lord's sustenance." Elder Hannah continued.

The what now?

The Elder was wearing that detached smile but her voice was firm. Something told Beth that they wouldn't be getting away so easily.

"We even just stopped at a restaurant to have dinner. We're fine, thank you for your hospitality." Beth said in the same firmness that the elder had spoken in.

"We insist." Elder Hannah said firmly.

Anna and Beth shared a look; they were definitely not getting out of this place without eating.

"Alright." Beth said through gritted teeth.

Elder Hannah just smiled her serene, saintly smile. "I officially welcome the two of you to the Unvaredonia Community."

***

Elder Hannah gave them a brief tour of the little town, she told them the story of how the community had come to be, how they gave up worldly possessions to live together as one big family. Apparently, they didn't trade with money and shared everything together.

"Just like the early settlers." She'd added.

She'd taken them to the little chapel where they worshipped and pointed out the toy and furniture factory. It was a quaint community that Beth might have appreciated if she wasn't being forced to stay. Anna said very little, leaving Beth to contribute to most of the conversation. Beth was a little worried about her sudden silence, she remembered Anna saying that she didn't like to engage in small talk – which was what this womxn was doing. But she'd engaged in small talk with Beth; was Beth the exception?

Beth felt her cheeks heat up at the thought of being considered special by Anna. She liked that she was the only one that Anna would open up to.

Finally, the tour was concluded and they were led to a slightly bigger house where apparently, the ten elders of the community lived in. Beth was hoping that they would march into the house and get started with dinner but the Unvaredonia had rules about dinner; dishes had to be arranged and seating arrangements needed to be made for their guests. Elder Hannah left Anna and Beth together in a small room that seemed like a living room of them. She spoke about going to inform the rest of the elders about their visitors and left Beth and Anna alone.

"That was weird." Beth said, immediately pacing. "This whole place is weird."

Anna sat down on a sofa and raised her palms up as if to say, what can we do about it?

Beth stopped pacing and stood in front of Anna. "What's up with you?"

Anna narrowed her eyes. For the first time, Beth realised that she couldn't tell what Anna was thinking. It was a little disorienting to be offered a door into somebody's life and then having your key seized and the door jammed in your face. That was how it felt to Beth.

"Nothing is wrong with me." Anna said.

"You're being quiet." Beth accused. She didn't like how she was feeling. In that moment, she could have easily substituted Anna for Carrie and it wouldn't have made a difference. Maybe Anna saw a little of that panic written on Beth's face because the look of indifference on her face eased away and a look of softness appeared. Beth thought that she might say something insightful or something that would immediately take away the edge that Beth was feeling.

"Nice skirt." She said instead.

Beth glanced down at herself and swore. "I thought we agreed not to mention the skirt." She said with mock anger, secretly she was glad that Anna was talking to her again.

Anna smirked. "I made no such promise, Beth, darling."

The term of endearment made Beth's chest glow with warmth. Anna seemed to have noticed what she said, she suddenly pursed her lips as if she could swallow her next words. Beth scrambled for something to say, she couldn't allow Anna to retreat into her shell again.

"You aren't supposed to make fun of the skirt. You're supposed to tell me how I would make a sack look like couture and how I look like a supermodel wearing this." Beth said. "It's like the number one rule of friendship."

"Friendship." Anna repeated the word with something akin to scorn. "You would make a garbage sack look like couture. You look like a super-model wearing this frumpy skirt." She said in the most serious voice ever, there was not a hint of amusement in her eyes as she spoke.

Beth found it harder and harder to hold Anna's gaze. There was a burning intensity in her eyes that scared her. It changed the dynamics of their relationship. Beth felt as if she'd known Anna an eternity even though it was barely six hours. She didn't want to put a name to what she was feeling.

Someone cleared their throat and Beth jumped in fright. She whirled around to face the doorway and saw that Elder Hannah was back. There was a new light in the womxn's eyes and Beth wondered how long she'd been standing there, watching the two of them. Beth wondered what she'd heard and what she was thinking.

"Elder Hannah." Anna greeted, standing up to her feet and coming to stand besides Beth. Was it just Beth or was there the slightest tinge of guilt in Anna's voice? As if she'd been caught doing something wrong. Elder Hannah smiled her usual smile but this time there wasn't any warmth in it. "It seems I misunderstood the two of you."

Beth and Anna exchanged a look.

"When you came into the shop, I thought that the two of you were friends. But it seems that you two are together, girlfriends?"

"NO!" Anna and Beth shouted the words with a vehemence that clearly startled the older womxn. She looked from Anna to Beth, not at all convinced and Beth realized why. The two of them were acting like teenagers who'd been questioned by the teacher and were pretending not to like each other even though it was clear as day to the rest of the people around them.

But it wasn't the case right now. Right? Beth didn't fancy Anna, she had a girlfriend of her own... It would be unfair to do this to Carrie and illogical too, she barely knew Anna, she hadn't known her up to a day.

She'd heard of whirlwind romance stories, one of her uncles had gotten engaged to a womxn he'd only known for a month. There was such a thing as love at first sight but this wasn't the case.

And Anna, there was no way Anna had feelings for her. She was too practical to develop romantic feelings for somebody that she just met, she was friendly yes but she hadn't shown any interest in Beth.

Except for that heated look she gave you a few seconds ago, her mind taunted.

Elder Hannah waved a hand. "I know what you might have heard about our community but we are generally very accepting. There's no use pretending not to be a couple when it is as clear as day that you're one." She said. There was a brief pause. "The way she looks at you." Her eyes were fixed on Beth as she said this.

A scarlet flush made Beth's cheeks heat up. This womxn was talking nonsense. There was nothing special about the way that Anna looked at her. The elder sighed as if she'd said too much already. "Anyways, there's no need to pretend. All that we ask the two of you is to abstain from any kind of romantic action while you're here."

Beth's cheeks could have fried an egg. She touched both hands to her face to disguise the obvious red. Anna was looking everywhere but at her, Beth looked down and found that Anna's fists were clenched tightly.

"All we require from you is chastity. No kissing." Beth saw how greatly it pained Elder Hannah to be the one to deliver the warning. Somehow, Beth managed to give her a curt nod.

The elder nodded. "Dinner will be ready in the next few minutes, I shall come for the both of you. Meanwhile, is there anything you require? Any allergies?"

Beth mumbled an answer while Anna said nothing. The elder gave them one final look before leaving.

The two of them stood, rooted to the spot. All Beth was thinking was that she wanted to kiss Anna, so bad. It was almost ironic that it had taken a stern warning not to for her to realise that she wanted to. It would be so easy to turn around and close the distance between them, pull Anna flush again her and press her lips against her.

She imagined how responsive Anna would be, she imagined deepening the kiss, she imagined letting herself take what she wanted for once, all consequences be damned.

Hot, Beth felt hot all over. She took a step away from Anna before she did something drastic.

"That womxn is crazy." Beth said in a shrill voice that didn't sound anything like her.

Anna was silent for a long time, then she took a step towards Beth and another until they were breathing in each other's air. She raised a hand as if to touch Beth's hair and then she let it fall back to her side.

"Tell me something, Beth. Tell me that I'm the only one thinking of how it would feel like if we kissed. Tell me I'm the only one aching to find out how our bodies would feel against each other. Tell me I'm the only one."

Beth could have done anything in that moment but she couldn't lie.

"You're ... she darted her tongue out to sweep her lower lip. Anna's eyes followed the motion. "You're not the only one."

Beth couldn't tell who moved first but one second they were standing in front of each other and the next she was melting into Anna's body, their lips fused together.

Anna grabbed a fist full of her hair, tugging her closer and closer as if she wanted to feel every inch of her. Beth kissed Anna back like this was the only chance that she would get. As if she would die if she didn't. A thousand different colours burst behind her eyelids. Her sensed amplified and heightened.

She let her hands wander until they settled on the curve of Anna's hips. She could have stayed like that forever, might have forfeited the urge to breathe again if it meant getting to kiss Anna until her last breath.

Her tongue danced with Anna's, hesitant at first but the two of them immediately settled into a sensual routine. Beth didn't want to stop. But as usual, all good things came to a fucking end, never lasting and always leaving a trail of devastation in their wake.

Someone cleared their throat and Anna wrenched herself away from Beth at a terrifying speed. Beth would later tease Anna about how fast she'd moved but now, she was only horrified that they'd been caught.

Elder Hannah was back. To the womxn's credit, she kept a poker face on, one wouldn't have thought that she'd seen anything at all. Her hands were behind her back and she stood, spine ramrod straight. She looked like a stern headmistress catching two rebellious teens doing something they weren't supposed to be doing.

Beth and Anna shared a look and Beth felt a little relief when she saw that Anna was fighting back a smile. They would deal with the consequences of their actions later, but all that mattered in that moment was that they were in it together.

Beth half expected an intense scolding from Elder Hannah, they'd after all broken a rule that they'd been given. Maybe it wasn't so bad, maybe Elder Hannah would kick them out and they could be on their merry way.

Without directions, her mind reminded her. But surely Anna was okay enough to drive now.

Elder Hannah didn't say anything, she only smiled wanly at them. "Dinner is ready. Come with me."

"Elder Hannah, we're so sorry." Anna began with an apologetic smile. "Maybe we should leave, just tell us the right directions to Margate and we'll be out of your hair."

Elder Hannah scoffed and waved a hand. "We already made too much for dinner."

Beth didn't miss the implications of her words. So if they hadn't made too much, she and Anna would have been escorted out. Beth wanted to take their bigotry and homophobia and shove it up Elder Hannah's stiff arse.

Anna nodded. "We're grateful for your hospitality."

Beth gave a little mocking bow on top. Elder Hannah eyed her as if she was a little slow. She spun on her heels without another word, clearly expecting them to follow.

"It's all your fault." Anna whispered to Beth, her voice was teasing and light. Beth relaxed immediately. Fine, something drastic had happened between them but they weren't going to make a big deal out of it. They were still Beth and Anna and they were in this together.

"How is it my fault?" Beth asked in false outrage.

Anna made a sweeping gesture at Beth. "I took one look at your skirt and I was seduced. You can hardly blame me for my lack of control."

Beth giggled. Elder Hannah tensed for a brief second but she didn't turn around, continuing to lead them down the dim hallway.

"I look ridiculous, don't I?" She asked.

She wasn't looking at Anna but she could tell that she was smiling.

"You're lovely, Elizabeth Granger."

They finally arrived in the dining room. About seven people were seated around the long table, each of them dressed similarly to how Elder Hannah was. There were two men while the rest of their hosts were womxns.

"These are our visitors." Elder Hannah announced. It was only then that Beth realised that neither of them had given the elder their names and it was clear that she didn't care. After all, they were only staying for dinner before leaving.

Beth and Anna murmured greetings to their hosts.

"Thank you for your hospitality." Anna added. Beth almost laughed at how impossibly polite she was being.

Beth noticed that there were three empty seats. One at the head of the table and was presumably Elder Hannah's seat. The other two seats were distanced from each other, one at the right end of the table and the other on the left.

Ah, so this was their punishment for making out with each other. Beth would have been outraged by the subtle homophobia but Anna gave her hand a quick squeeze and she smiled.

She silently vowed to herself to be as subtly unbearable throughout the dinner. Their hosts deserved the very best level of petty.

***

There was somebody knocking on the door. Carrie startled awake as the knock grew louder on the door.

Where the fuck was Tiff?

Oh, right. They weren't at Tiff's place anymore. They'd eaten takeaway and decided to go to Carrie's place in Soho. Despite the fact that Carrie was technically moved into Beth's place in North London, she still kept her apartment, actually Beth covered the rent monthly.

Carrie had given her a speech about how she didn't want to feel as if she was leeching off Beth and needed her own place, in case Beth ever got sick of her. The guilt trip had worked well, Beth got sad every time Carrie brought up their financial difference so she'd agreed when Carrie said she wanted to keep the apartment, she'd offered to pay rent too. Carrie hadn't even needed to hint at it too much.

The flat was a scrappy flat that was small and entirely hers. It was where the real Carrie lived; the Carrie that loved to have friends over without ever consulting Beth, the Carrie that smoked weed and got wasted.

She hadn't been over at her own place for weeks now, since the last time she'd thrown a party. The place had been the same as she'd left in when she stepped through the door an hour ago.

She and Tiff had gotten to cleaning up the place, then gave up half-way and decided to smoke instead. She must have fallen asleep sometime in the last thirty minutes. The pounding on the door caused her head-ache to worsen. She rolled over to the side of the bed and found it cold.

Huh, where was Tiff? Was she one knocking?

Carrie groaned and stood up, she grabbed her shirt off the floor and wore it. She left the small bedroom and walked into the adjoining living room. She carefully avoided stepping on the cans of beer still strewn around the space.

She opened the door and found a scowling Tiff on the other side.

"Did you want to bring down the fucking place? The door wasn't locked." Carrie snapped.

Tiff brushed past her, wet hair sticking to her shoulder and smelling of Beth's orange scented shampoo. Carrie had taken the bottle of it from Beth's place to use for herself.

"The door wouldn't open from the outside." Tiff answered. She turned around to look at Carrie with something akin to disgust. "You are still wearing yesterday's clothes. You should shower and then we'll take a walk."

"You sound like my mother." Carrie grunted.

Tiff rolled her eyes. "Didn't she never give a fuck about you?"

"Neither do you," Carrie pointed out but she was already walking away to the bedroom and then the bathroom for a shower. She stripped out of her clothes and got under the shower, yelping when cold water poured down on her. She heard Tiff's laugh echo from the living room.

Carrie muttered expletives under her breath, she couldn't remember the last time she'd taken a cold shower; the bathroom in Beth's house always had hot water. She soon got used to the chill and took her time washing off the grime and smell of alcohol on her skin. She poured a dollop of the shampoo on her palm and rubbed it on her hair, humming under her breath.

She finished her shower and searched through the single wardrobe if she had anything to wear. Tiff was wearing some of her clothes so there had to be something for her to wear in here. She found an old pair of leggings ripped at the knees and a baggy t-shirt. When she returned to the living room, she caught Tiff smoking a cigarette.

Carrie shook her head at her. "You're going to give yourself cancer."

"And you. Did you know that most people that get lung cancer get it from the smokers in their environment? You should be worried about yourself, Car." Tiff said but she crushed the cigarette on the table in front of her and stood up. "Ready to go?"

Carrie narrowed her eyes at her bubbly persona. Tiff was acting a little weird. "What's the problem? Why are you in a hurry to leave this place?"

Tiff scrunched up her nose in obvious disgust. "It's absolutely disgusting in here. I can feel it clogging up my pores." She kicked at a can of beer. "Are you going to clean this place all by yourself? Because I'm not helping."

There was a half open pizza box on the lone couch in the living room and that was perhaps where the stench was coming from. Carrie sighed, maybe she could guilt trip Beth into giving her some money so that she would hire some cleaners to clear the place, "Definitely not."

Tiff smirked knowingly, there was something a little off about it but Carrie couldn't figure out what, besides, she was still too tired and hung over to overanalyze anything. Maybe some fresh air would do her some good. She gave Tiff a nod, "Let me grab my phone," She said.

Carrie returned a second later and gestured at Tiff to lead the way. There was a man waiting outside the building when Carrie came out. She recognized him almost immediately.

She swore under her breath. "Shit. Tiff turn around, we're going back inside." But Tiff was a little too slow. "Why? What's going on?"

The guy looked up and caught Carrie's eyes. Now, it was too late to run. Carrie plastered a fake smile on her face as the guy approached her, a deep scowl set on his face. He looked like he wouldn't take no for an answer this time.

"Hey, Ryan." Carrie greeted. "My man."

"Cut through the shit, Carrie." He snapped. He held out a hand before her. "You owe me two hundred pounds, let's get straight to the point."

Carrie barely noticed Tiff hovering nervously behind them. She licked her lips, trying to gain control of the situation. The landlady lived in one of the flats and she disliked Carrie; the only reason that Carrie hadn't been evicted yet was because she was likely the earliest tenant to pay rent. "Keep it down, there's no need to make noise about this." Carrie hissed. "I already told you that I would give you the money when I've got it." Usually, that would appease Ryan. Carrie didn't owe him money often, she usually paid for whatever she bought from him. This was one of the few times and it was because of that damned party that she threw weeks ago. She'd gotten some stuff from him and promised to pay back within days but days had become weeks and he still didn't get his money.

Carrie had made sure to be far from the house, she thought that he would forget about it or that she'd pay him when it was convenient for her but from the looks of it, that hadn't worked well.

The dangerous glint in his eyes told her that he wasn't going to leave this time, no he wasn't going to make it easy for her.

CHAPTER *ELEVEN*

Dinner was mashed potatoes, steak and a side of green peas and a glass of water; no wine in sight. Anna didn't know why she was surprised. These people were a community that aspired to return to the simplest state possible because they thought that it would make them better than the rest of the world.

She glanced down at her plate, at the generous portion on it. She didn't have any appetite for food, not only had she eaten less than an hour ago, her heart was still racing from kissing Beth. If Anna closed her eyes, she could still taste Beth on her lips, could still feel the crush of her chest, her hand on Anna's hips. The rush of colour that had flashed through her mind in the moment that her lips met Beth's. How could she possible return to normal life after that?

She now understood why people were addicted to getting a high from drugs; if this euphoric feeling coursing through her veins was the same feeling as a being high, Anna was willing to be addicted to Beth. She forced herself to return to the present, they were in the presence of their generous but strange hosts. The sooner Anna played nice and convinced them to give them directions to Margate, then the faster they got to leave this weird sanctuary.

Anna stabbed a pea with her fork and popped it right into her mouth, as if on Cue Beth did the same thing; their eyes met across the table and simultaneous smiles spread on their faces – barely contained. Their hosts however were not impressed. A stern faced man at the other end of the table glared at Anna.

"We haven't said grace yet." He chided. Oops.

Anna wondered if she should spit out the pea in her mouth. She decided that it would be disgusting, so she swallowed. "Sorry, I'm not religious." Her parents hadn't been so Anna had never stepped foot into a church, had never been curious enough to even try one. She wondered if Beth was religious; the chances of that were low, judging by the scorn in which Beth had spoken of religious people. That was one more thing that they had in common with each other. Anna smiled at that.

"Before any meal, you ought to close your eyes and say grace." Elder Hannah took over the chiding from where her companion stopped.

"Sorry." Anna said. She was surprised when Beth didn't apologise, she carefully chewed on her pee and swallowed. When Anna's eyes met hers, she winked slowly.

"I'll say Grace." One of the nameless female elders said. She linked her hands with the elders besides her and Anna too spread her hands to be held. She felt paper rough skin on hers and felt the urge to shudder. She didn't really like being touched. "Let's close our eyes." The elder added as an afterthought.

Anna obliged and the womxn began to pray. Anna didn't pay attention to a single word, she felt Beth's eyes on her and cracked one eye open. She swept her gaze over the whole room, making sure that nobody was watching her – all eyes were closed in devotion, except for Beth whose blue eyes were wide open and twinkling in amusement.

Anna fought back a giggle, especially when Beth winked again.

"Absolutely ridiculous." Beth mouthed.

"Absolutely." Anna mouthed back. So this was what it meant to be ridiculous; following a bunch of rules and having a permanent stick up one's arse. It was definitely not a lifestyle for Anna. She'd stick with going to hell for her beliefs or rather, lack of one.

Beth made a funny face, mimicking Elder Hannah's stern look. Anna sent her a warning look; she would be dragging Beth down with her if she had to go down. Something told her that Beth wouldn't care very much. Anna had to admit, there was something different about her.

It wasn't very obvious but it seemed to Anna that Beth was learning to stand up for herself and not take anyone's disrespect lying down. The Beth that Anna had met this morning would have apologised to the Unvaredonia elders meekly, she wouldn't have wanted to do anything that would upset her host but not this Beth; this Beth wasn't taking anything lying down.

Anna felt hope strike a match in her chest; this Beth would be well equipped to handle Carrie. Finally, the prayer came to an end and Anna muttered a quick Amen with the rest of them. The elders dug into their meal, not with gusto like Anna expected; they ate slowly, as if deliberating the food, judging it like chefs would do in the cooking shows. They showed no emotions on their face, no sign that they were enjoying the food before them. Anna stabbed at her steak and tried to mimic the mannerisms of her host. The food wasn't bad by any means – Anna had had better steak but it wasn't terrible. She didn't think that she would finish it all. Looks like they would have to offend their hosts either way.

The sound of cutlery clanging on the fine china was the only sound in the room. Anna normally found silence peaceful, welcome even but she felt a little uneasy now, maybe because the elders were watching them very keenly and making no attempt to hide that fact.

Just when Anna thought she wouldn't be able to stand the silence again, one of the elders spoke – a wiry thin womxn wearing spectacles. "Where are you two from?" She asked.

Anna and Beth's eyes met. When Beth didn't make any attempts to answer the question, Anna did.

"Well, we're both from London. I work as a property solicitor in a law firm while Beth is in real estate and property." Anna answered. Not that she expected a round of applause from them, but she was taken aback when the elder scoffed, a quiet sound barely audible but Anna caught it anyways.

"Lawyers are often soulless people. They represent foul organisations wanting to expand on their wealth. Nobody needs that much money." The womxn said, she spoke rather dispassionately about the topic as if she'd talked about it a thousand times before.

Anna agreed about the wealthy companies wanting to buy out smaller businesses but she didn't agree that lawyers were soulless people. She took another bite of her food.

Beth however smiled, there was nothing nice in it. "I hardly think anyone is in a position to judge. Casting the first stone and all that." Beth said.

Anna hid her smile behind the pretence of drinking her glass of water. The elder shot Beth a mild look but didn't latch on to the bait. "I hear that the two of you got lost on your way to Margate. However did that happen?"

Beth hopped on the question before Anna could answer diplomatically. "Anna was driving but she had a few too many drinks."

All eyes turned to Anna, there was a palpable shock in the air. Beth might have well called Anna an alcoholic. "She's a stickler for the rules and refused to drive. So I took over and I'm terrible at driving, I missed a few turns and we wound up here." Beth spread out her arms as if she was describing some grand journey.

"How long have you two known each other?" Elder Hannah asked with a tight smile. Anna heard the unasked question; how long have you two been together?

"Two years." Beth answered quickly. She shot Anna a sly look. "We've been together for two years."

A pin could have dropped in the room and it would have been heard. The silence was tension filled because despite Elder Hannah's spiel about same sex relationships being accepted by the community, the truth was that there wasn't much acceptance. Barely any at all. They would rather Anna and Beth pretend to be best friends; you can be gay but don't rub that stuff in my face. Basically it meant that they needed to pretend to be straight.

After Beth's answer, none of the other elders made any attempts to quiz them. They ate their dinner in the same slow, infuriating manner. Anna just continued to stab at her plate, raising her head every few moments to smile at Beth.

CHAPTER *TWELVE*

"Let's try to get through this like civilised adults." Carrie said, trying to adopt an air of calm. She tried not to shiver in broad daylight because of the determined glint in Ryan's eyes. She didn't know him that well – a friend had introduced them – but she had heard the rumours of how he'd been part of a knife gang and that he'd once stabbed someone. He definitely wasn't someone to be messed with but Carrie had unwittingly messed with him. She didn't have two hundred pounds on her. The truth was that Carrie was in a whole lot of debt, she owed too many people and for the most stupid things, thinking back on those situations made her want to hit her head on the wall several times. She barely had enough in her card to pay for her and Tiff's lunch and whatever was on that credit card wasn't up to fifty quid – enough for her next meal and then it was back to the apartment she lived in with Beth.

Beth would be appalled that Carrie was in debt and even more appalled to know that Carrie had dabbled a little into gambling in the past few months; well, more than a little gambling. It had started out harmless enough, just a little bet on games with friends then it was more than that – worse, she was borrowing money to place bets.

Now, here she was.

"Don't fucking talk to me about being civilized adults." Ryan spat out, jabbing a finger at her. He didn't look like much; he was middle aged and beefy. He kept the silliest looking moustache that Carrie had made fun of many times behind his back. But, he was far bigger and stronger than her.

At least they were in broad daylight, surely he wouldn't do anything to her while other people walked by. Surely all the knife stabbing rumours were just that – rumours.

"I want my money now." Ryan said, he reached out and pushed her slightly and if it wasn't for Tiff behind her, Carrie would have staggered to the floor. She shrugged herself out of Tiff's grip.

'What the fuck?" Carrie screamed. Her heart beat in a tune to fear and anger. "You can't just go around pushing people."

Ryan tried to push her but she sidestepped out of the way and he almost careened into Tiff. He growled in frustration and turned around.

"You bitch!" He screamed and grabbed her arm. Carrie tried to shake him to no avail, his grip was iron on her upper arm, which was certainly going to leave a bruise. Carrie cried out in pain when he twisted.

Tiff hovered behind the both of them uselessly. "Fuck, you guys stop." As if they were two middle schoolers having a toss on the field during recess.

Ryan raised his free hand, fist clenched and in the air, headed straight for her face. Carrie cringed, just when she thought that he would hit her, a clear voice shouted from the balcony above them.

"Hey, what is going on here?" It was the landlady, a cranky lady in her late fifties. She was the nosiest person Carrie had ever met; always trying to poke her nose into her tenants' business. The damned womxn would always complain about the parties that Carrie threw as if it was any of her business. Still, Carrie had never been so glad to hear her nasal voice. Surely the sight of her would send Ryan running away.

Ryan didn't immediately let go of her but his grip on her arm loosened a little.

"It's your bloody arse again, always ruining the neighbourhood peace." The landlady croaked a laugh that turned to a few seconds of hacking coughs. The damned womxn wouldn't let go of a cigarette for one day, she clearly had other things to worry about but no, she chose to focus on other people's business. She leaned on the bannister and scowled down at the three of them. "I won't allow you to cause problems on my property. Get the hell out of here, all three of you."

What the hell? This wasn't going the way Carrie had expected.

"This isn't over." Ryan pointed a thick finger at her.

Carrie looked up at her landlady, expecting that the womxn might defend her for once. The old lady gave a derisive snort but she didn't say anything. Carrie didn't dare breathe a sigh of relief until he was out of her line of sight.

"I said all your arses to get the hell out." The landlady's voice came again, this time booming loud and startled Carrie.

Carrie blinked up incredulously at her. "I live here."

"No, you come here every few weeks and throw wild parties and wreck my building." The womxn shot back. Carrie flinched at the venom in her tone. "And you're owing rent." The womxn gave a sudden snort as if finding humour in something that only she knew about.

When Carrie remained rooted to the spot; partly in shame and fear, the landlady barked at her this time all traces of amusement wiped clean off her face.

"I said get the hell off my property before I call the police on you."

The mention of police had Tiff tugging on Carrie's arm. Carrie shrugged off her grip.

"I can walk on my own." She hissed at Tiff. She looked up at the landlady for what might be the last time and flipped her off with both hands. She didn't bother waiting for the aftermath.

***

After what seemed an eternity, dinner came to an awkward end. None of the elders attempted to make any more conversation after Beth's bold answer; best not as if they were unwilling to hear the cold, unfiltered truth. Then again, Beth hadn't exactly told them the truth about her relationship with Anna. They weren't together by any stretch of the word; they had known each other barely one day and all they'd shared was a kiss. There was a lot that hung in the air about their future together or a lack of one anyways. Plus, their journey to Margate had been temporarily postponed by Beth's detour to here, if all went well, they would still be visiting the house. The house where Beth planned to start a new life with Carrie; her girlfriend.

Anna barely caught herself from frowning obviously. She settled for clenching her fists by her side. She didn't want to think of Beth with

Carrie; laughing with Carrie or kissing Carrie. It would have been ironic if it wasn't so painful, of course it was exactly like her to fall for the first person she managed to have a connection with. All her life, Anna had stuck out like a sore thumb, her difference in personality clear to everyone around her. She'd been shunned for it and eventually, she had stopped trying to be socially acceptable, stopped trying to get what other people clearly did.

She had sugarcoated the truth to Beth concerning what happened with her last relationship. They had dated for four months before her ex-girlfriend said Anna was too cold for her. "You're like a robot, it's scary." She'd said matter of factly, uncaring if she hurt Anna or not. Or perhaps she'd been so blunt because she thought that Anna couldn't be hurt; that she felt no emotions. Just like a robot.

In hindsight, Anna couldn't remember just what she'd liked about Whitney. The two of them had met at the convenience store of all places. Anna couldn't even recall what she'd been buying then but Whitney had been ahead of the line to pay and had been short five quid to pay for her groceries. Anna had handed her the money without a second thought. Whitney had been grateful and offered to repay Anna back in some way. Even then, Anna should have known that the two of them would have never worked together. Whitney had been an exact polar opposite; her hair when they first met was a bright blue that was almost childish. She had favoured wearing brighter colours too that matched her bubbly behaviour. She'd insisted on paying Anna back some way and in the end, Anna had given her phone number so that when Whitney finally thought of some way to pay back the five quid, she'd give her a call.

A week later, Whitney invited her to come over to her flat for dinner, Anna having much free time to herself had said yes. Dinner hadn't been half bad, Whitney predictably dominated most of the conversation. Most people didn't find Anna's quietness alarming the first time; they thought she was a challenge, someone to coax out of a shell. Others thought she was a great listener. Until said quietness made them uncomfortable. Whitney soon grew bored of hearing her own voice all the time; she'd wanted someone adventurous, someone who got up at 2am to watch the stars. Anna wasn't that someone.

So she'd grown bored and dumped Anna after getting a job somewhere far away. Anna hadn't exactly been heartbroken because she expected it and maybe a part of her had been using Whitney. Misery did love company after all.

Here she was again, falling for the first person that gave her attention. Except, Beth wasn't Whitney. And Anna was stuck in an impossible situation with Beth. She wasn't sure that she was going to make it out of this with her heart unscathed.

She put on a brave face though, trying to pay attention to what Elder Hannah was saying. Even though dinner ended in an awkward note, Elder Hannah had offered to show the two of them on a tour; more specifically of the toy factory. Why she thought that Anna and Beth would be interested in seeing a toy factor, Anna didn't understand but they still needed to get directions from them.

Beth was nodding along to something the Elder was pointing at. All of her earlier defiance seemed to have disappeared, she was back to showing polite interest. Despite that, Anna saw that Beth was charmed by this quiet, recluse community; the sense of togetherness that one could never find in the city. The truth was that Anna was a little charmed to. She could imagine herself making a life somewhere like this place; just her and Beth, they would only have time for each other, surrounded by like minded people. The two of them could be themselves, no need to hide or pretend to be people they were not; Beth would be herself – stubborn and freely so, she would speak her mind without being afraid that her words would be used against her. And Anna would love her, the way she deserved to be loved.

Anna shook her head, she was getting lost in a fantasy again. She realised that they'd crossed to the other side and were in front of the toy factory. It was a small suburban house with picket fences surrounding it. It looked like a normal home to Anna, she could imagine a normal family living within those walls.

Elder Hannah must have noticed the looks on their face because she was quick to explain. "All our furniture and the toys for the little children are handmade by a skilled carpenter. A man who has been part of our community for years, he used to be a banker if you can believe that."

Beth couldn't hide the wide eyed look of disbelief on her face. Elder Hannah smiled.

She spread her arms a little. "It's hard to believe, I can tell. If you see him, you would never guess that he used to be one of you." Although Elder Hannah didn't say the word with scorn, there was a firm draw on the word. She definitely thought that all city people were soulless people or at least people on the path to trading their souls away. Anna wondered how many years she'd been part of the community and who she'd been before it. She tried and failed to imagine this nun like womxn as a city womxn, in fact, trying to conjure an image of Elder Hannah wearing jeans and a nice top almost made Anna giggle.

She looked at Beth and saw that she must have been thinking the same thing; she too looked like she wanted to laugh.

Elder Hannah pushed the small gate and crossed the lawn to the front door. Anna and Beth hurried after her. She pushed open the door and stepped into the house. It was a little disorienting adjusting her eyes from the sharp afternoon sun to the dimness inside. Distantly, Anna heard what must be the hacking of a saw on wood. The curtains were drawn close and Elder Hannah immediately headed to remedy that. It was like a flower blooming the way sunlight filled the room.

She saw that they were in a living room but it was mostly bare. There was a circular coffee table in the middle of the room that was made of wood − their host's handwork it seemed − and a rocking chair in the corner.

Elder Hannah turned to them with a blissful smile. Anna was instantly wary of that smile, it was kind of creepy. Anna was pretty sure that the womxn didn't like either of them much, she was likely putting on the appearance of friendliness because her beliefs said so or something.

"Gilbert often loses himself in his work and is likely upstairs." She announced and with a sweeping gesture, she urged Anna and Beth to mount the staircase. The floorboards creaked loudly with every step on it, Anna winced, thinking that it felt like the floorboards were groaning from the effort of bearing their weights.

Elder Hannah led them down the short hallway upstairs, there were three doors on each side and she opened the last one on the right. Anna was pleasantly surprised by the tall windows that allowed the sun in, casting shadows on the floor. The room smelled strongly of paint and was crowded with furniture; rocking chairs and half finished cribs, a large shelf dominated the right side of the room − displaying rows upon rows of wooden figures; some were dolls and others action figures.

A man was in the middle of the room, slightly hunched as he sawed into a thick log of wood. He looked up when the door opened and Anna found herself thinking that he was quite the character. For one he had no eyebrows; they were shaved off, giving his slightly bulging eyes a comical look. However, the deep set of his jaw was unsmiling.

He wore a stained, dark blue apron over the plainest looking tunic and trousers – the same drab colour as Elder Hannah's garment. Anna wondered if it would be offensive to ask if the Unvaredonia coordinated their outfit colours or if they'd taken some kind of oath against nice looking colours. There was no way to politely frame that question so she didn't ask, besides, she was already known for saying the wrong things and pissing off people; she'd stave off that instinct until they'd safely gotten directions out of this weird place.

"Sorry to interrupt, Brother Gilbert, but we have guests." Elder Hannah addressed the toy-maker, she gestured at Beth and Anna. If Brother Gilbert had any eyebrows, they would be furrowed in confusion; the skin where his eyebrows were supposed to be was wrinkled together.

Clearly the Unvaredonia community didn't get visitors often. It was hard to wonder why.

Anna didn't think that Brother Gilbert interacted much with people, judging by the way he was regarding them warily. Suddenly, she was consumed with curiosity to find out why he'd chosen to join the Unvaredonia.

"Nice to meet you," Beth said after a moment of silence. It was obvious that Elder Hannah had been waiting for them to introduce themselves to the toy-maker. What happened to making the introductions like a normal human being?

Anna was both irritated and amused by her behaviour; it reminded her of being in middle school and her teachers doing everything to make sure she got along with the other kids. Those attempts never worked anyways.

"You made all these?" Beth asked rhetorically, she gave a slow spin, taking in the whole room. Anna tried to see it from her eyes and she found herself being infected by some of Beth's enthusiasm. It was kind of amazing, that one man had made all these with his hands – Elder hadn't mentioned anything about a partner assisting him. "You're very talented."

Although the toy-maker didn't smile, his stance seemed to soften. There was no mistaking the clear and genuine awe in Beth's voice. She very obviously appreciated this man's skills and he could tell.

"Thank you." Surprisingly Brother Gilbert's voice didn't sound rusty. He enunciated his words just fine, with a hint of carefulness but he sounded fine. He wasn't quite the reclusive character she'd built in her head. Anna bit back telling him that.

Stay polite, she chided herself mentally.

Beth crossed her hands behind her back in a way that reminded Anna of a kind schoolteacher; the kind that took an interest in your work and offered constructive criticism; she certainly looked that way in her floral top and the weird skirt she was wearing, all that was missing was the tortoise shell glasses perched on her nose. She might make a good teacher too, Anna thought.

"Elder Hannah told us that you used to be a banker." Beth continued in a conversational tone but there was a hint of mischief in her voice that Anna smiled. Elder Hannah's smile dimmed a watt and Anna's own smile grew. She didn't know what Beth was up to but if she planned to upset the uptight older womxn, then Anna was solidly behind her and willing to aid and abet.

Poor Brother Gilbert looked taken aback by the mention of his old life.

"A long time ago, wasn't it?" Elder Hannah cut in with a shrill laugh. What was she so afraid of? That the toy-maker would reminisce on his old life and want to return? He was after all a valuable asset to the community, Anna bet they would hate to lose him.

"How long have you been in Unvaredonia?" Beth asked.

Brother Gilbert abandoned all attempts at sawing his wood, he was probably afraid that Beth would shock him with another of her questions and he'd end up cutting off his own hand. He began to polish a shelf of figurines with a stained rag. He was silent for a few seconds and Anna got the sense that he was just surprised that he was being asked about a past he'd willingly left behind. For a brief second, Anna's conviction wavered, maybe it wasn't right to quiz this man like this. She didn't like to talk about her past, surely this man felt the same way.

But Brother Gilbert didn't appear offended, his back was turned to them but he could have rebuked Beth's question if it so offended him.

"A decade." He finally answered, his voice was tinged with something like nostalgia, for his old life or for something in his old life? It was a little difficult to tell.

Anna was thinking how it was usually easy for her to get a read on people; she might not be good at social cues but she was good at telling what kind of person someone was. She'd easily known that Carrie was a horrible person – she would have been able to tell even though she hadn't witnessed their fight in the bathroom. She'd easily known that Beth was a good person, she'd been able to see through her insecurities. But she was finding it hard to get a read on the toymaker. Something told Anna that he was like her; weird in the sense that not many people got them.

She shook her head, a little amused. If someone had told her that she'd spend today falling in love with a womxn she just met and spend her day in a weird, exclusive community and relate to this burly man with no eyebrows, she wouldn't have believed them. She might have even paid for their psyche evaluation. She wasn't a believer in fate or any of her counterparts but this had to be some cosmic joke from the universe.

"That's a long time." Beth was saying. The toymaker hummed a non-committal answer.

"How did you make such a big decision to uproot your life?"

Maybe it was because Beth sounded so genuine with her question that the toymaker decided to answer her. Even Elder Hannah, who Anna expected would rebuke Beth for asking such a question appeared curious, as if she too wanted to hear the answer.

"Love." The toymaker answered. Anna was startled by the answer, she tried to catch Beth's eye but for once, her whole body was turned to the toy-maker, her desire to know his answer running through and true.

Anna felt something cold slither down her spine. Was Beth asking for herself? Although Margate wasn't exactly an isolated community like the Unvaredonia was, it was still a huge change from the hustle and bustle that London was. It was quieter for sure, the perfect escape from the madness of the city. If Anna was being honest, the idea of leaving the city didn't sound bad at all. Had Beth already made up her mind about moving? Perhaps the final push that she needed was whatever the toy-maker would tell her.

"Love?" Beth echoed, sounding a little disbelieving.

The toy-maker turned around and hung his dusty rag on one of the posts of a crib. He didn't quite smile but there was the slightest twitch of his lips. "Not in the way you think of, miss. Elder Hannah must have told you that I used to be a banker in the city. It was a soulless job and I hated every bit of it."

His voice was fierce and his eyes took on a faraway look, likely imagining himself working behind a desk in an office that offered a stunning view of the city. Not such a hell, Anna thought but didn't those usually differ with each person? Currently, her own idea of hell was watching Beth be reunited with Carrie — she even shuddered at the thought — it was totally valid that this man's own version of hell was working a nine to five job.

"I fell into depression, all my friends deserted me. I picked up carpentry then and my love for it bloomed, it became more than a hobby and more of something that I'd been destined to do." Brother Gilbert explained in a gruff tone. It must have been a long time since he'd spoken of his past to someone.

Once again, Anna found herself being jealous of this passion that people spoke of. Beth talked about the same discovery of her love for carnivorous plants and Anna had heard countless other discovery tales. It would be nice to talk about something inanimate with so much love.

"The city was sucking my soul and I knew I had to get out. I got in my car and just drove away, without a certain location in mind, all I knew was that I needed to leave, needed to put this passion first. I stumbled upon this accepting community and the rest is history as they say it." A different person might have spoken with such flair but Gilbert's words were raw and simple. They seemed to resonate with Beth.

"Thank you for sharing your story with us, Brother Gilbert." Elder Hannah said with a solemn nod, as if they were at an Alcoholics Anonymous meeting.

"Thank you." Beth said softly. "And you never regretted it for once?" She asked after a brief moment.

Anna watched Beth's face; the slight curve of her lips as if she was recalling something. A memory with Carrie?

Jealousy was a sharp stab in Anna's chest.

Brother Gilbert shook his head. "Never. Love doesn't regret."

What a load of crap, Anna thought bitterly. She was feeling a little regretful, if only she'd stuck to her job description, she wouldn't be here, thinking of how it was going to hurt like a storm when Beth broke her heart. She noticed that Elder Hannah's gaze was on the two of them, a little wary and something else that Anna couldn't identify.

Beth didn't ask any more questions and Elder Hannah swooped back in, showing off Gilbert's creations. Beth oohed and ahhed at the right times but Anna was too distracted to muster much enthusiasm. She just stood in the corner and watched the sun from the window. After what seemed like an eternity, the tour came to an end and all three of them left the toy-maker's place.

Beth asked if the toy-maker interacted often with other people.

"He's very dedicated to his work." Elder Hannah said; she seemed to be walking towards the clothing shop that Anna and Beth had met her in. "He likes making toys for the little children but he prefers his own company."

Anna believed that. Perhaps she was right that the toy-maker had been misunderstood throughout his life, like she too had been misunderstood by plenty of people. But he wasn't exactly like her, Anna was lonely even if she didn't like to admit that. The toy-maker however, liked being alone, being with his love. Anna had nothing like that.

"Thank you for your hospitality today." Beth told Elder Hannah. Her cheeks pinkened. "Even though we weren't the perfect guests." Just by looking at Beth's cheeks, Anna could tell that she'd been referring to the kiss.

Blood roared in her eyes as Anna replayed the kiss over and over in her head. Until it was a movie montage and she was in control of the remote. She pressed rewind on the moment that her lips touched Beth's. The press of their bodies together and how Beth was so, so soft against her own body; it was the sweetest kind of torture.

Anna cleared her throat, "Yes, thank you. For lunch and the tour. I've previously heard about the Unvaredonia community but today I've learned plenty about you and your people."

Elder Hannah wasn't the type to beam; she gave a nod and a smile. "We're merely doing what the Lord told us to do unto strangers."

They crossed the street and entered the shop.

"Can I keep this?" Beth gestured to her skirt. "I would really love to pay you back in some way."

Elder Hannah waved a dismissive arm. "Pay it back to some other person in need." It was an answer so predictable that Anna smiled.

"And now, for your directions." Elder Hannah said, clasping both hands in front of her.

***

Five minutes later, Anna and Beth were back on the road. Beth was looking out the window as the road zoomed by. Beth held out her hand on Anna's thigh. It took everything in her not to lose control of the vehicle in that moment, even though it was an innocent touch.

Get yourself together, Fenwick, she chided herself mentally.

"Want to tell me about it?" Anna asked. She was both disappointed and relieved when Beth removed her hand.

 Was she going through her hormonal teenage phase? She'd skipped that when she was a teen in secondary school, while other kids were new to sex and getting it on in the most awkward places, Anna had been mostly uninterested. She had her first kiss in her last year of high school with the most popular girl in school who'd been closeted then – Katie Hall had been too scared to confront what it meant that she was attracted to girls, she'd liked keeping Anna on the side, claiming to have feelings for her but being part of the people who would mock her at school. Anna had been exhausted with the back and forth so she'd broken things off between them. Her first time was in sophomore year of college with her first girlfriend.

The truth was that Anna was wired differently; she didn't feel attraction to people unless she actually liked their personality and was comfortable with them. Yet, it had taken all of one day to like Beth and want to kiss her until she was dizzy.

Beth's voice snapped her back to the present. "It's the whole day in total. It feels like weeks instead of barely seven hours." She laughed softly. "I feel like I've known you forever."

There was a field of daffodils closing in the distance. They were Anna's favourite flowers; the one that her mom used to get a big bunch in every weekend. Anna barely registered that she'd killed the engine of the car. It was as if Beth didn't notice that Anna had stopped driving either. The two of them just gazed at each other.

It was so easy for Anna to get lost in Beth's eyes. She didn't know when her hand reached out of their own accord to cup Beth's cheek. She wondered if it would be too cheesy to tell Beth how beautiful she looked, even while she was wearing that ridiculous skirt.

She waited a beat, for Beth to pull away, to stop her. There was no sound but the distant chirping of birds and their own breathing, syncing with each other. Anna almost confessed there and then. To keep the words from escaping too soon, Anna sealed Beth's lips with her own.

***

They were back at Tiff's apartment. Carrie was pacing the length of it, agitated. She paused to point an accusing finger at Tiff who was sitting down.

"You told Ryan where to find us." Carrie said bitterly. It was the first word she was speaking to Tiff since they arrived at her apartment half an hour ago. There was nobody else that could have told Ryan where Carrie would be except Tiff. Sure, there was the probability that Ryan had been staking out her apartment for days, weeks even but that required a lot of dedication that he couldn't afford. He definitely wanted his money, but Ryan was too busy selling stuff to other people to visit her apartment several times in a row. It had to have been Tiff. Carrie could visualise it clearly; maybe Tiff had run into Ryan somewhere, he must have recognized her and perhaps even threatened her to set up a meeting with Carrie. Even though Carrie would have done the same if she'd been Tiff, she couldn't help but be stung by Tiff's betrayal. Not that Tiff seemed to care about the hurt and anger written all over Carrie's face – neither of them were deluded enough to make the mistake of developing feelings for each other, their relationship was purely physical and maybe a bit of camaraderie because they shared similar upbringings. Other than that, there was nothing.

Tiff sat, eyebrows furrowed in wariness but there was not a hint of apology on her face. At Carrie's words, she gave a helpless shrug. "Don't act like you wouldn't have done the same thing, Car. Don't be like this." She said coolly.

"Like what?" Carrie shot back, her voice raising a little.

Tiff barely concealed a look of contempt. "Pipe the fuck down or you'll get me in trouble with the other tenants."

It was clearly the wrong thing to say. Carrie gritted her teeth, trying and failing to reel in her anger. "You got me in trouble with my landlady, what the fuck am I saying? You got me evicted from my apartment."

"Because you owe rent." Tiff snapped. She leaned back against the sofa and crossed her arms over her chest.

At that moment, Carrie couldn't help but think of Beth. If this was an argument with Beth, Carrie would have won by sheer intimidation alone. Beth was soft spoken and she balked at the slightest confrontation, always looking to Carrie for reassurance that their relationship wasn't hanging on the ropes. Even though Beth was the one with the influential family and the wealth, Carrie very obviously wore the pants in their relationship. But Tiff wasn't like Beth, not at all. She was more like Carrie, which meant that she knew all her manipulation tactics and wouldn't stand for any of them; hard to fall prey to a trick that you invented yourself.

Suddenly, Carrie wished that she'd gone to Margate with Beth and the lawyer. Beth would likely be miserable without her and if she'd been with Beth then Ryan would have never found her and Carrie wouldn't have argued with her landlady..

She ran a hand through her hair. "What does me owing rent have to do with the fact that you lured a dangerous man to my flat?" She threw her hands up in frustration as if Tiff didn't still get the picture.

Tiff finally lost her cool. "It's not totally my fault, okay!"

Carrie stopped pacing in front of her. "Then whose fault is it, Tiffany?" She spat.

Tiff shot up from her seat. "Don't you dare use that tone of voice with me. I'm not your needy emotional girlfriend that you can just bully around and get away with it."

"And stop denying that you're a snitch!" Carrie shouted, exasperated.

Tiff flinched, she shook her head. "Look Carrie, when it comes to covering your ass at the detriment of mine, I'm sorry, I'm not going to do it – no matter how good you are with your tongue."

A snort escaped her lips. "And you just defined snitching but you continue to deny it."

"Ugh," Tiff sighed loudly. "Fine, Ryan cornered me at the convenience store. I was scared and I panicked okay. It'll all be fine if you pay him what you owe."

Carrie rolled her eyes. "Are you in middle school, Tiff?"

Tiff ignored her words. "Just pay him the money." Her lips curved in a sinister smile that had Carrie immediately on her guard. "Unless you're lying."

"About what?" Carrie feigned a breezy laugh.

"You said you didn't want to go to Margate with Beth, or was that what actually happened? Or did Beth ask you not to come with her?" Tiff asked in a sly voice. "Maybe she changed her mind about the joint ownership."

"Don't be ridiculous." Carrie snapped. "Beth begged me to come with her. I said no because I didn't want to. She'll do whatever it takes to keep our relationship going."

Carrie didn't realize that she'd fallen right into Tiff's trap until she saw the smirk spread wide.

"Go ahead." Tiff urged, jerking her head at Carrie's phone on the table between them. "Call her and ask her for five hundred quid."

A cold shiver snaked down Carrie's spine. She wouldn't lie and say that she hadn't thought of calling Beth. But the truth was that, a few weeks ago, Beth lend her a thousand pounds. They'd rowed for days before Beth agreed to lend her the money – a lot of guilt trip had gone into convincing her too. And in a matter of two weeks, it was all gone. Beth would surely ask where the thousand pounds had gone in such a short time.

And that would raise a bunch of questions that Carrie didn't want to answer. Tiff probably knew that, judging by the wicked twinkle in her eyes. "I'll text her." Carrie said, hoping that the bravado in her words would be enough to get Tiff to back down. They weren't. She just gestured at the phone until Carrie walked and picked it up.

Just as Carrie's fingers hovered above the virtual keyboard, Tiff's voice cut in, "Don't text her, call her." Tiff glanced down at her bare wrist. "They should already be in Margate; perhaps they're taking a tour right now. She'll be too occupied to notice a text, it is best you call her." How Tiff managed to disguise the glee in her voice for concern was likely something that should be studied. Carrie wasn't fooled because she knew better.

"Sure, I'll call her." Carrie replied in the same saccharine tone. Tiff only smiled.

Carrie dialled Beth, putting her phone on speaker so that Tiff could hear. With each ring that went unanswered, the smirk on Tiff's lips grew and Carrie felt her cheeks heat up in embarrassment.

"She's probably taking the tour." Carrie told Tiff, trying to speak in a breezy, nonchalant tone that she wasn't sure she conveyed well.

"Hmm." Tiff hummed in mock agreement. "Maybe you should call again; it'll get her attention this time."

Carrie did. She called three more times but Beth never answered. She didn't even register the look of victory that Tiff wore on her face. Cold fear slithered down her spine. In the past, Carrie was perfectly content going days without seeing Beth or even talking to her, sometimes she would make up nonexistent events that she needed to attend alone, artists retreats, meetings with important people that didn't exist. Beth was usually quite understanding – she never nagged when it came to Carrie's work. Carrie usually took advantage of that understanding to make even more outlandish claims; once, she'd lied to Beth that she was going on an artists' retreat for two weeks and that the event was supposed to help artists be in tune with the great outdoors and that phone calls from the outside world was banned. She'd known that Beth found the thought of no communication for weeks frightening but she'd lied anyways.

However, throughout Carrie's own constant deceptions, Beth had been nothing but faithful and understanding. Even on the rare days when Beth had to visit a far away location for her family's real estate business, she still kept in touch, called as often as she could. It wasn't like Beth at all to miss Carrie's calls. Especially when Carrie needed her the most now.

Indignation rose bitter in her chest, maybe Beth was trying to punish her for not going to Margate. And only hell knew what kind of ideas that solicitor had put in her head – Carrie didn't trust Anna Fenwick one bit. There was something far too clever in her eyes that Carrie didn't like.

She might not know a lot of things but she was pretty sure that Anna Fenwick had crossed the line from professional to personal when she'd stopped Beth from signing the joint ownership document. It was also at her insistence that Beth agreed to go to Margate. Carrie couldn't understand the meddling.

She hated to imagine all the things that she might be filling Beth's head with. The last thing Carrie needed was Beth developing a spine out of nowhere. Not when Carrie needed her, or more accurately, needed her money.

"I'm going to text her." Carrie said aloud, more to herself than to Tiff who was still watching her keenly.

If Beth wanted to play hard to get all of a sudden then that was fine by Carrie. She could grovel a little, say the right words that would have Beth thinking that Carrie had been body swapped by aliens. She thought for a second, fingers hovering above the keyboard before she swiftly typed a message.

How's Margate? I miss you, please call me.

Then she pressed send.

***

Distantly, Beth could have sworn that she heard her phone vibrating but her mind was a wild fest of sensations. Anna's lips tracing down her neck, her hands, firm and roaming. Beth's own hands shoving Anna's jacket out of the way and then their lips breaking away from each other for a long moment as Beth's hands shakily but surely unbuttoned Anna's blouse. Their eyes met, desire a kaleidoscope of colours melting in Anna's stormy gray eyes.

Are we really doing this? Beth wanted to ask. Perhaps it was some kind of fever dream that Beth had conjured up. Any moment from now, someone would call her name and she'd snap back to the drab, colourless present.

Beth undid the final snap of the button and Anna's lips was back on hers. Beth let out a breathy moan. If this was a fever dream, she didn't ever want to wake up.

CHAPTER *THIRTEEN*

Anna wouldn't exactly describe the silence as awkward; for one, it really wasn't silent. The radio was one, turned to some top 40 hits sunset segment and was playing an alternative song from the latest album of a female jazz singer. The volume was low enough that Anna couldn't make out the lyrics but the tune was both honey to her ear and hammer to her heart, that Anna might have found herself crying if it was some other time – that was if she wasn't focused on Beth's presence. There was only so much watching one could do while driving – which was very little unless she wanted to get the both of them in an accident.

It was hilarious thinking now that she remembered that she'd passed her driving test with high scores. Her instructor had praised her for her 'intense' concentration. Ironic, because it was a battle keeping her eyes solely on the road. She wanted to drink in the sight of Beth until the image of her was burned in her mind. She bit her lip, recalling the sounds that Beth had made, the softness of her body.

Anna clenched her thighs together as subtly as she could without Beth noticing. She was thinking of something casual to say, something that would break the sudden tension between the – partly of the sexual nature. She groaned in her head, thinking that this was exactly why she stayed away from casual physical relationships. They weren't her style and despite what happened with Beth half an hour ago, she still wasn't interested in casual relationships.

She wanted all of Beth with an intensity that scared her. And would likely scare Beth too if she found out. Anna forced herself to inhale a deep breath. There was no need for her brain to go into overdrive like this yet. If she, the cool and calm thinker was having such internal panic, she couldn't imagine how Beth was feeling; Beth who liked to wear her heart on her sleeve, who bore a lot of insecurities and liked to second guess herself because of the years of emotional abuse she'd suffered from the people that were supposed to love and protect her.

This wasn't the time to panic. Anna blew out a slow breath. They were approximately ten minutes away from the house, having already arrived in Margate. It was every bit the seaside town that Anna had imagined, nice houses, quirky outdoor pubs, and small town businesses. There was a certain charm to it that Anna immediately fell in love with. She risked a sideways glance at Beth but her face was turned away. She was however, jiggling her thigh at a speed that was frantic.

Against all logical reasoning, Anna reached out and touched a hand on Beth's moving thigh. Hurt caused a pang in her chest when Beth immediately flinched away from her. Anna tried not to feel too bad about it, after all things were very much complicated between them.

Neither of them had embarked on this journey expecting it to go this way; that they would end up developing feelings with each other and end up having intimate lovemaking in Anna's convertible car, next to daffodil field. If Anna didn't already have an unhealthy attachment to her car, then she definitely did now.

So maybe Beth was feeling a little jittery; she was allowed to seeing as they were on a drive to the house that she'd inherited from her late aunt – something that she hadn't yet come to terms with from what she'd said earlier. There was also Carrie.

It took everything in Anna not to groan aloud at the thought of that womxn. To Beth, Margate was going to save her relationship with Carrie and they'd live happily ever after. Anna had been hoping that their detour, the moments they'd spent together this afternoon would be able to remind Beth of the carefree womxn that she used to be; and open her eyes to seeing the kind of person that Carrie was. Anna still wasn't sure if she'd succeeded on that front. Now more than ever.

"Just try to calm down." Anna said softly.

Beth tensed even more. She finally turned to look at Anna, her cheeks were flushed a satisfying shade of pink. Anna almost smiled until she realised that the wide of Beth's eyes wasn't in glee but in guilt. Her heart dipped into her stomach.

"We need to talk about what happened, Anna." Beth said, she tried to sound stern and firm but her voice wobbled as if she was going to cry. She sighed heavily. "I can't believe that happened." She bent her head between her palms and Anna knew that nothing had changed.

***

Carrie shut the door behind her, feeling as if a thousand years had passed since she'd last been in this apartment when in reality, it had only been a few days since Beth had been pissed off that she left a water bottle in the hothouse. Even though Beth lost her cool, she'd still apologised in the end, she'd been willing to do anything to fix the rift that she thought was growing between the two of them. That Beth would have done anything. This current Beth was ignoring her calls and leaving her texts unread.

Carrie walked further into the apartment, she kicked off her shoes and pushed them with her feet underneath the shoe rack by the door. There was no Beth here to chide her anyways. Carrie walked away from her shoes but a second later, halted in her steps. There was a nagging voice in her ear telling her to fix her shoes on the rack – and the voice oddly sounded like Beth's.

Carrie shook her head defiantly. "You don't bloody tell me what to do." She snapped at no one but in the end, she went back to her shoes and arranged them on the rack. Surely she couldn't be missing Beth, she didn't even care about her – all she needed was money.

She could never miss Beth; who was likely having a swell time frolicking around in fucking Margate. She snorted, it probably wasn't even possible to have fun in Margate. What did people even do there for fun? She didn't even like that city's artists community.

She got herself a bottle of beer from the fridge and settled on the arm of a sofa. She cracked it open with her teeth and took a swig of it, her mind drifting back to Margate.

Margate sounded like the kind of place that Beth would like; quiet and away from the city. Carrie wasn't still keen on living in the middle of nowhere but it wasn't sounding like such a bad thing now. Sure, it was still boring but if she promised to move there with Beth, surely she'd pay off her two hundred pound debt too – it was mere change to Beth. Everyone would be happy; Beth because Carrie agreed to move and Carrie would jointly own the house in Margate with Beth. If she ever got bored, she'd make up an artist retreat or several – maybe a trip to abroad if she liked.

Carrie drank again from the bottle, feeling slightly cheered up. If only Beth would text her back.

She took her phone from her pocket and texted Beth again. Ryan would never find her here; even Tiff didn't know where she lived with

Beth; Carrie had always been careful to keep some aspects of her relationship with Beth from Tiff. It wasn't that Tiff would pull stunts out of jealousy, well, she was jealous but of Beth and not because of Carrie. She would be safe here from everybody. All that was left to do was to wait for Beth to reply to her texts or call her back. Preferably within the next hour.

CHAPTER *FOURTEEN*

For the life of her, Beth couldn't understand how she'd gotten into this situation. Things were moving fast; too fast that her head spun from the dizziness of it. Now that she thought about it, she'd never been on a trip that spun so wildly out of control before.

After graduating from secondary school, she'd gone on a trip with a few friends from class; they'd gone in a rented car since none of them had cars of their own but halfway into the journey, the vehicle had broken down and they'd been stranded in the middle of nowhere – they'd had to call a towing truck and then been refunded half of their money from the car renting company who had previously promised them a smooth journey. Beth and her friends had spent the extra cash on paying for a bed and breakfast. Their journey had been cut short and the next day, their parents came for them – that was the story she usually told people when the topic of wild road trips came up.

But this was wilder than anything else that Beth had ever experienced. She imagined meeting up with her cousins to catch up and telling them that her girlfriend had ditched her mid journey into looking into the house which they might potentially end up moving to, that she and her solicitor had gotten drunk, taken a wrong turn and ended in a reclusive community. To top it all, she'd tell her cousins that she'd ended up shagging her solicitor in her nice convertible.

She could only imagine all the jaw that would drop; Beth had done a few wild things in college but nothing that extreme. There was nobody who knew her that wouldn't be surprised that she'd ended up sleeping with a womxn that she'd barely known a day.

What is wrong with me? Beth thought. She flushed, thinking of what had just occurred in the car. She didn't think she could ever look at a convertible the same way anymore.

"Gosh, I can't believe that we did that." Beth said with a slightly hysterical laugh.

She wasn't surprised when Anna didn't laugh. She dared to sneak a glance at Anna's face and saw that she was frowning intensely, her grip on the steering wheel tighter than before. Perhaps she too was thinking of how foolish they'd been. She waited a beat, for Anna to say anything, interject with a joke like some people would – Beth had had a few one night stands herself, she knew the drill – but Anna wasn't most people and more than ever, Beth found it near impossible to tell what she was thinking.

With the tension growing between them, Beth found herself growing more and more nervous, trying to block the thoughts from rushing in or the implications of things. She'd slept with her lawyer and it might be the most wonderful thing to happen to her but at the same time, she was feeling a thousand other different feelings. She couldn't try to make sense of them because she didn't quite understand them herself either.

She silently willed Anna to say something but she was silent.

"Is this part of the job description?" Beth blurted out. The quick way that Anna whipped her head to stare at Beth would have been comical if she didn't almost lose control of the car as she took a particularly dangerous swerve on the road.

"Eyes on the road!" Beth screamed.

Anna regained control as swiftly as she'd lost it, she gritted her teeth and shot Beth a steely look. "I am looking at the road."

"Are property solicitors allowed to do this? Are they encouraged to sleep with their clients?" Beth gave a shrill laugh, she was making a joke, wasn't she? But her insides were cold with the thought that this was Anna had been playing some twisted game of duty all along.

Anna was silent for a beat. Another, then, "If you'd like to get to the house in Margate in one piece, then I suggest that you stop saying things like that, Elizabeth Granger." Anna's voice was tight with barely concealed outrage.

Beth felt a ridiculous relief course through her veins. "My bad." She said, interlocking her fingers together and releasing them again. She wasn't quite sure where exactly to look; at a very furious Anna or outside where every second that passed, every zoom past a building meant that they were closer and closer to the house. Beth would have to confront what she'd been running from.

Anna shook her head, as if she couldn't stand the apology. She blew out a frustrated breath. "I thought you knew me, Beth. I thought..." She trailed off. "No, it's not part of the job description. I'm a property solicitor, not a whore."

Beth flinched at the rawness of Anna's words and perhaps that was a bit of hurt she detected in Anna's voice. "I'm sorry."

Anna didn't seem to hear her, she talked right over Beth's apology. "My firm doesn't whore me out to the most expensive clients and ask me to sleep with them to ensure that their every need is met. I don't do casual flings and hookups, I never have – since you're bringing it up."

"Anna--" Beth tried again.

"What happened between us happened Beth; stop trying to pin it on me, it takes two to tango." She ground out.

Again, Beth flinched. She wanted to cover her ears with both of her hands. She didn't consider herself a prude by any means and she wasn't about to start acting like one. But Anna's words were forcing a reality upon her shoulders, one she didn't want to confront yet. Maybe even ever. Because then she'd have to wonder why she made out with Anna. Why she'd cheated on her girlfriend of three years. In the years that Beth had been with Carrie, she'd never once thought of cheating – not when Carrie frustrated her or even when she felt the weight of unhappiness on her shoulders. She'd never thought of leaving or cheating. But in just a day of meeting and knowing Anna Fenwick, Beth had thought of what it would be like if she was with Anna instead. In less than a day of knowing Anna Fenwick, Beth had slept with her.

"Oh, god, what have I done?" Beth breathed out. She felt sick to her stomach, overcome with the urge to throw up everything she'd eaten, to erase the taste of Anna on her lips and the feel of their bodies pressed together. "What have I done?"

She raised her head up slowly. She was suddenly grateful that Anna was driving, it meant that she didn't have to make eye contact.

"We made love." Anna answered matter of factly.

Beth cringed. "Please don't say that."

Anna wore a look of stubborn defiance on her face. "You can't bury the truth no matter how desperately you might want to."

"Stop!" Beth shouted suddenly.

Anna quietened immediately, there was a look of hurt and incredulity in the wideness of her eyes. She must have realised that this was the first time that Beth had raised her voice.

Beth tried to regain control of the situation. "You can't talk like that, Anna. What happened between us was a mistake, a blip in time if you will. We have a professional relationship and our purpose for this trip was purely professional too." She didn't give Anna a chance to interject, she quickly added, "We let things get a little too casual; getting lunch and getting tipsy. Yes, we both needed to wind down." Even to her own ears, it sounded like she was trying to convince herself. "That was it, that was all it was – a mistake." She added firmly and looked away from Anna, not wanting to see the look of devastation that would appear on her face.

She told herself that she was trying to spare Anna from heartbreak but her lie wasn't even convincing to herself. Beth was being purely selfish and it was breaking her heart.

***

Susan was in her study, looking at a framed photo of her son when he was five. In the picture, she was bent slightly, to wrap her arms around his waist and rest her head softly on his own. It was one of the few photographs of him that she could stand to look at. The later pictures of his teenage years made her feel nothing but deep, aching grief that kept her up at night. When she looked at those pictures, she searched for the signs she'd missed, perhaps there was some sort of clue in those pictures that could have let her know that he was suffering the way that he did. In the end, it had been too late to tell anyways.

When he died, she'd thrown herself into her work, important research that could help other people like him. It was supposed to be a form of psychoanalysis that caused the patient to go into a dream like state where they would relieve their memories, earliest to present. The psychedelic trip could change one's entire outlook on life, causing them to reevaluate and come out with a totally new perception of life. If she'd known what she did now, maybe she would have been able to save her son from the depression that killed him. Her work was important and she wasn't ashamed of it, not in any form at all. Even though it might be condemned; even her peers didn't have such belief in her work. When Susan had first started out early research on it, she'd asked a few of them to embark on the research with her but they all thought it was problematic and unethical.

Now, Susan was growing more optimistic in it. If only she didn't have the problem of the new landlady visiting. Somehow, she didn't think the landlady's reception of her experiment would be positive. She might be appalled or worse, think that Susan was running something highly illegal. The other tenants thought that the best course of action would be to keep Simon away from their visitors but Susan didn't know if that would be entirely possible.

Maybe it was time that the truth was revealed. She wanted her research to help people but it wasn't going to do much help if kept the details hidden forever. Susan set the picture back down on her desk; she distantly noted that the desk was messy, papers were strewn across the surface, including a few textbooks. She was very busy in recent days and was always postponing arranging the office. She could have asked Felicity or Nancy to do it for her but nobody ever came into her study – it was her sanctuary in the way that the garden was to Nancy. She'd have to do it herself.

She thought that she might just do that, tidy up the place a little. She started to stack together some papers when her eyes strayed to the clock hanging above her seat. It was a few minutes to five pm. It was almost time to check up on Simon. She couldn't believe that she'd let herself get distracted and miss checking up on him as she usually did in the evenings. If she wasn't afraid that setting up her study in the same room that he was in would disturb the experiment then she might have done so just so that she could keep an eye on him all the time.

The early stages of this experiment had been boring to say the least, nothing happened apart from the occasional REM – she remembered being excited when that had first happened. Now, she was just wary and close to pessimistic; she'd never anticipated the trip taking such a long time this time. What if Simon didn't wake up this time?

Susan shook her head and tried to force herself to remain rational. She was a scientist; there was no time to let emotion and bias cloud her thinking. She set a heavy stapler on the neat pile of papers that she'd just arranged so that they wouldn't be caught by a breeze and then she went on her way. She heard Felicity and Nancy chatting up in the garden behind the house. She halfheartedly wondered where Hunter was. None of them particularly worked but Hunter used to work as a handyman and sometimes headed out to help their neighbours fix leaking pipes.

She reached the room where Simon was in and twisted the knob quietly, the door creaked open and she winced at the sound. When she entered the room, she wasn't surprised when she saw that Simon was still asleep. For a few seconds, she watched the steady rise and fall of his chest – reassurance that he was still alive but that wasn't much reassurance in recent times anyways. Was it possible for one to sleep forever? Susan supposed that they were about to find out.

Susan already had a few theories why it was taking so long for Simon to wake up this time around. When she'd met Simon and Felicity a year ago, they had been on the verge of divorce. Simon had been dealing with depression and a lot of self loathing, so much baggage that he thought he deserved.

Through his internal conflict, he'd wanted more than anything to get better for Felicity and to save their marriage. When Susan had presented the idea of her work to him, he'd regarded it with cautious suspicion. Even while Susan explained to him that he wouldn't exactly be healed but that the experiment would cause him to confront his trauma from his earliest memories to the present as an adult.

"That might take a while," He'd joked dryly. "I have a lot of issues to sort through." He'd been joking then but Susan wondered if Simon's trip was taking so long because there was simply too much mental turmoil to sort through. Susan wasn't a neuroscientist by any means but she was curious to know how if his brain activities would be going haywire.

She clenched her grip around the notepad she was holding. This was why she needed this to work, she had the sense that she was on the path to creating something historic.

She walked closer to him, observing his form for a few seconds before she carefully took his vitals; all appeared to be well on that front, he was breathing steadily and his heart rate seemed fine too. Susan frowned. Apart from rapid eye movement, there was no sign that he was actually on a mental journey, surely whatever Simon was experiencing in his dreamlike state ought to transmit to his vitals – a spiked heart and pulse rate perhaps.

Susan bit down on the end of her pen – a bad habit she'd developed in college that she'd never quite been able to rid herself of. She continued to stand at the foot of the bed, watching Simon. At one point, she began to count each rise and fall of his chest. She noticed it almost a little too late; a slight stutter in his breath every few rise and fall of his chest. At first she thought that she'd imagined it but she watched again and caught it happen.

Susan moved closer to him, barely even registering when she hit her knee against the bed frame. Simon did it again and this time, clenched his fists – the action was so quick that she could have blinked and missed it.

Her heart soared with hope. She hurriedly scrawled down words on her notepad without daring to take her eyes off his form. This was progress; it meant that Simon was close to waking up. It was only a matter of hours, and then, Susan was going to find out the extents of change that he'd undergone.

This was the breakthrough she'd been waiting for and it was going to change the course of everything. There was no way she could keep this to herself anymore, keep the details within the confines of this house.

A few minutes later, she'd gathered the rest of the group in the living room. They all wore varying looks of apprehension on their faces; she could only imagine what they were thinking. The day had been a rollercoaster of emotions – mostly panic – and it wasn't even over yet.

"Have they called to say they aren't coming anymore?" Hunter asked in a voice that was cautiously optimistic.

"Have you decided to settle with them? Are we going to move out?" Nancy asked. Of all of them, she looked the angriest, Nancy and Hunter had dealt with a few issues with their previous landlords and it had ended with them chucked out on the streets, they hadn't been able to afford a lawyer to sue. Susan had found them and the rest of it was history. Nancy was the last person that would agree to back down without a fight.

"Calm down and listen to the womxn first." Felicity chimed in, she smiled but it was a little strained. Of all of them, she was decidedly more worried about Simon since he was her husband.

"This isn't exactly about the house." Susan began. She saw Hunter's quizzical stare and answered, "And no, they haven't called to cancel the trip so they're presumably still coming."

Susan smiled. "That is what I wanted to talk to all of you about. Simon is waking up in a few hours."

Happiness exploded on their faces, Hunter whooped and hugged his arms around Nancy's obvious bump. Felicity was a bit more subdued about her joy; her eyes shone with tears of relief. Susan supposed she should be offended that they'd been so obviously worried about Simon but she was too happy to bristle at their disbelief.

Susan explained the recent developments to them, they attentively listened, nodding carefully. She was struck with a wave of affection for all of them. They'd trusted her and continued to do so, even when her own peers had scoffed and balked at her ideas. But Hunter asked questions about her work even though he didn't know the first thing about psychoanalysis, Nancy always brought her tea and a sandwich on the days that she got lost in writing the theoretical analysis of her research. She only hoped that they would support her now.

"That's great news." Hunter said, he was smiling. "I'm really curious to see how Simon's trip has affected his relationship with mortality, surely, reliving."

Here came the demanding part that they might not be so enthusiastic about. Susan took in a deep breath, "Which is why I want her to know about it."

The silence that followed was confused. It was Felicity that dared to ask. "Who's her?"

"The landlady coming over today." Susan replied calmly.

To their credit, there was no massive meltdown or shouting. They all knew better than that anyways, the house had ruled – they communicated with each other in responsible tones, airing out their grievances if they had any rather than bottling them and bearing simmering resentment against each other.

"You can't be serious." Nancy said, shaking her head from side to side. "That's crazy!" She added.

"We don't use abusive words in the house, Nancy." Susan chided gently.

"It is certainly not wise to do that, Susan." Hunter cut in, standing up from the sofa he'd been sitting on earlier. "I don't think this is a friendly visit for one. We've lived here for almost a year and even after the old landlady died, this new one didn't show up. We don't owe rent and suddenly, they want to visit."

"Yes! They're going to show up wanting to evict us and they'll be looking for anything incriminating to pin on us. Susan, your research is important but it is illegal. You could go to jail; we could all go to jail." He continued, gesticulating wildly. The mention of jail was enough to cause Nancy to panic, she held her belly tight as if she was afraid that the landlady was coming for her baby too.

"And what about Simon? About Felicity? You can't make this decision without considering them."

At the mention of her name, Felicity tensed. All of them waited for her to say something, she just stared at Susan, silently giving her the go ahead to continue talking. Susan cleared her throat just right before Hunter looked like he would launch into another spiel, "We are a community and all your concerns are very much valid."

"But I'm tired of keeping this project under wraps, like I'm ashamed of it when the truth is that I couldn't be prouder of what I've come up with – what all of you have contributed to. I'm not ashamed of my work and I want them to know about it and maybe if I explain it to them, they could realise that everything that we're doing here is good."

Nancy scoffed. "I'm sorry, Susan but this is madness. You know that not everybody has been accepting of your work, we're not asking you to be ashamed – we're equally as proud as you are but there's a lot of hate and greed out there, what's to say that these people won't go right ahead and report you to the nearest police station?"

"You can't trust them. We should be making plans of how we'd keep any paraphernalia out of the way; keeping your study off limits and Simon out of sight. That is what we should do." Nancy said firmly, she turned to face Felicity and took her hands. "And I think I speak on behalf of everyone in here."

For a brief moment, Susan thought that Felicity might say something to contradict Nancy but in the end, her hesitance and desire to protect Simon won out in the end. Nancy faced Susan again, there was not a hint of smugness in her face, she wasn't arguing against Susan's suggestion for the fun of it or to assert some kind of dominance but because she thought that she was suggesting what was best for all of them. Nancy had been pushed over by landlords enough times that she wouldn't allow it again and this time, not to people she considered family.

***

Anna had known that this was coming; she'd known that her dalliance with Beth would end in nothing but pure, sweet pain but she was still shocked by how much it hurt that Beth hadn't chosen her, worse, by all the accusations that Beth had thrown around. As if they hadn't come to know each other in the past few hours. She remembered that Beth was likely used to this; she'd gone off the rails in university after all desperate for one last taste of freedom, she would have had enough experience with breaking hearts. Anna would be another notch on her belt, it seemed.

If Anna had any ounce of dignity, she might have quit now, accepting Beth's cop out in silence. If she wasn't in love with Beth, she'd nod and agree that everything that had happened between them was nothing but a mistake, a lapse in judgement and then she'd drive Beth to Margate, they'd tour the apartment and she'd take all of Beth's notes into consideration. She'd let Beth sign the joint ownership document with Carrie and then she'd walk away and act like nothing ever happened.

But Anna was in love with Beth, so much that it killed her to imagine Beth signing her happiness away by staying with Carrie. Too much that her fear that Beth would let Carrie continue to bully her trumped her fear of laying her heart bare for it to get trampled. So she was going to do exactly that, lay her heart bare, try hard to hold on to Beth even though she could feel her slipping far and farther out of her grip.

"Listen to me, Beth. You're not getting the last word here, so just listen to me." Anna said, she tried to make her voice sound firm and unyielding but the truth was that there was a quiver mixing in with the confidence she tried to project.

Beth gave a watery laugh. "Why are you so stubborn? Why won't you just let this go?"

Anna mimicked the same laugh. "It's one of my few endearing traits."

Beth shook her head, "They're not few. Oh, Anna, you're a wonderful person." She seemed to realise what she'd said because she suddenly clamped her lips shut. Anna was beginning to see beneath the hints of defiance, even though she might not admit it out loud, it was breaking her to do this. So why was she adamant on torturing the both of them?

"I'm not the kind of person to play games. I've been straight forward with you," Anna said, she killed the engine because she didn't think she could get through this conversation without getting them into an accident.

Five fucking minutes, they were approximately five minutes away from the house. Anna had five minutes to convince Beth to choose herself. Because this wasn't really about Anna being with Beth, it was about Beth realising what kind of womxn she was, that was what this whole trip about, the detours, all the strangers that they'd met. Anna was thinking of Brother Gilbert who'd left a toxic workspace to do what he loved; to be who he was. Beth needed to pick her own self, above a three years toxic relationship that was doing nothing but take and take away from her – a situation Beth didn't want to leave because of a sense of duty and loyalty. Because she was afraid.

"I would never do that to you, I have too much respect for you to do something so stupid. This trip meant the absolute world to me, knowing you is the best thing that has ever happened to me; I've been living in a world of grey before I knew you and now there's just so much colour that I never want to go back and I know that it has to be the same for you."

Beth was shaking her head vehemently. "I can't, Anna. You don't know me."

"I know what I need to know. The past nine hours say otherwise. You don't need an eternity to know someone, maybe all you need is proximity and getting away from the rest of the world. I know you more than I know myself, I know your fears, your dreams, your hopes – I know that even though your parents tried to kill it, you still hold on tight to your love of plants."

"Don't be ridiculous, Anna. This could never work." Beth tried to say.

"I know you!" Anna shouted because she felt like if she didn't repeat the words over and over again, then Beth would never understand the implications of the words. "I know your heart, your head and your body."

The flush that overtook Beth's face was the most beautiful thing that Anna had ever seen.

"Anna, stop, okay. I'm with someone, I have a girlfriend and I can't do this to her. What do I tell her? She would have been on this trip with us, she would have gone on the same adventures that we did. And I just forgot about her and let things get too far, but it's gone far enough. If

Carrie found out, it would break her. Her parents have already let her down, this would be a slap in the face from someone who's supposed to love her the most." Beth ranted, she jabbed a finger at Anna. "I'm with Carrie. I love her and she loves me and that's it."

Anna's mocking laugh echoed in the space of the car. A womxn walking her dog along the sidewalk across the street kept glancing at the car, Anna had brought up the roof of the car but the windows were transparent and they certainly could be seen arguing.

"Of course it all boils down to poor Carrie." Anna sniped.

Beth flinched and Anna immediately regretted the words, she didn't apologise though but she meant them. Surely, Beth must know that Anna didn't like Carrie.

"I don't appreciate you speaking about my girlfriend like that." Beth said coldly.

Anna knew that she was tiptoeing on dangerous grounds, all day she'd skirted around telling Beth the outright truth about what she thought of Carrie because it was too premature to say anything yet, because she didn't want to push Beth away yet. Now, she was up to her neck in frustration.

"Surely you can tell that Carrie isn't the perfect partner. Beth, you're a lot of things – most of them amazing but you aren't an idiot. Carrie isn't a fucking child, she's an adult who should be able to own up to her trauma and not use it as an excuse to have others pity her. And most of all, she doesn't love you, not like..." Anna trailed off.

The look on Beth's face was nothing short of murderous. "Not like what?"

Anna raised her chin up, she might as well say it, she'd come this far after all.

Just as she was about to utter the words, Beth's phone rang. She snatched it off the dashboard and Anna caught the name on the screen; CARRIE. Speak of the proverbial devil.

***

Carrie was surprised that Beth answered this call this time that she almost dropped her phone.

"Car?" Beth's voice came, a little impatient but Carrie got the sense that the impatience wasn't directed at her. For a moment, Carrie said nothing, feeling relief course through her veins. Beth hadn't abandoned her after all and everything was going to be fine.

"Babe?" Beth's voice came again, none of that impatience present. She sounded like the normal, sweet Beth that Carrie knew.

"Sorry, I'm sorry. I'm still here." Carrie finally spoke. The both of them were silent again and Carrie got the sense that each of them had dealt with hell today and were wondering how the hell things had gone so wrong in a day that was supposed to be normal. Carrie certainly had come within inches of her life – maybe she was being a little dramatic but she was going to be in huge trouble if she didn't pay Ryan the money that she owed him.

She briefly wondered what the hell had gone on with Beth's trip to Margate.

"Are you alright?" Beth asked. "How did the meeting go?"

Carrie almost blurted out, "What meeting?" Then she remembered the excuse she'd given Beth so she could get out of accompanying Beth to Margate. Gosh, that seemed so far away now, like it had happened a lifetime ago.

"Oh, it went fine. I'm at home now. I miss you." Carrie said. She felt a little awkward saying the words, perhaps because they were untrue.

Another pause. Then, "I miss you too, babe." Why did Carrie get the sense that Beth was lying too?

She shook her head, maybe Ryan had ruffled her more than she thought if she was imagining nonsense. Beth loved her and she would do anything for her, she'd been desperate for Carrie to come along this morning. Things didn't change that fast and people didn't stop loving each other in a matter of days.

Carrie inhaled a deep breath. "How's it going there? You should be at the house now." She couldn't have sounded more disinterested but as usual Beth didn't notice.

"Um, actually, no." There was expectant silence after Beth's answer and it took a moment for her reply to sink into Carrie.

"You aren't in Margate yet?" Carrie asked, incredulity shining in her voice. "The drive to Margate is two hours tops even if you find yourself stuck in traffic. It's been more than seven hours." Carrie fired back accusingly. She imagined Beth cringing at every jab and sighed, this wasn't going to work if she didn't make an attempt to be pleasant to Beth.

"Sorry," Beth's voice came quietly. "There were a few unanticipated stops. The car broke down once or twice." She added quickly, too quickly. Carrie narrowed her eyes, she knew Beth enough to know that she was being secretive about something.

"That solicitor can't even do one thing right, huh?" Carrie couldn't resist one last scathing remark. This time, Beth didn't say anything. Carrie cleared her throat; sheesh was she so used to being mean to Beth that she couldn't summon the smallest iota of politeness? "Are you okay though? I know you're desperate to see the house today."

Beth huffed a tired laugh. "I'm fine, don't worry about me, Car. And yeah, it would be nice to see the house today."

This was where Carrie was supposed to interject and declare her intentions to join Beth. Somehow, she felt the words getting stuck in her throat. Come on, just say it, she chided herself internally but the words refused to be uttered. Carrie felt as if she would be trapping herself to proverbial eternal damnation by moving to Margate, it didn't matter that Ryan was probably going to send her to literal eternal damnation. Moving to Margate felt like conceding to allowing Beth to control her forever.

But Carrie needed the money, she just needed to play along for a little while and then she'd have her freedom.

"Is it too late for me to join you there?" Carrie finally forced out.

Dead silence. Not even Beth's breathing.

"Beth? Are you there?"

Nothing. Then, "Are you being serious right now?"

"Beth? I asked if it was too late for me to join you at Margate? I'll commute there in no time at all, I shouldn't have bailed so fast like that but your insistence scared me. You know how much I don't like the change."

"I'm sorry, I didn't mean to pressure you." Beth said.

Carrie was barely listening, already swept up in her charade, already in character. Sometimes, she thought that she should have been an actress.

"But fuck it, you're my girlfriend. I'll move halfway across the world for you and with you."

Beth was silent again and Carrie bristled, it wasn't as if she'd expected an ovation over the phone and Beth declaring her undying love but she'd expected a few sniffles, maybe Beth telling her that she felt the same and for her to get on the quickest train right this instant. It seemed that she was getting none of that.

"Car, are you sure? I don't want to force you to do something that your heart isn't in." Beth said, picking her words carefully. Carrie felt a shiver of fear run down her spine. That sounded like a rejection to her.

"Do you not want me there?" Carrie snapped. "I'm saying that I want to be with you and you don't even believe me."

"What? NO." Beth backtracked. "I want you here, it's what I want."

"You aren't acting like it." Carrie retorted. "Don't tell me that womxn has put ideas in your head about owning the house in Margate. First she didn't want us to sign the joint ownership contract together and now it's something else. Maybe she's told you that you can do so much better than my poor arse."

"Carrie, please don't be like that." Beth sounded on the verge of tears and Carrie didn't bother to tamp down on the smile that spread on her face. Beth was starting to sound like the Beth that she knew.

"I'm going to come meet you then." Carrie announced breezily.

"I can't wait to see you, love." Beth said softly.

Carrie didn't deign her with an answer, she hung up and put her phone besides her on the sofa. She stood up and decided to get changed before she left the house. In a matter of hours, everything would be all fine and dandy in Carrie-land again. Carrie already felt better thinking about it.

***

Listening in on that call definitely ranked as the worst moment in Anna's life. Even though she hadn't been able to properly make out Carrie's words, she'd heard her yelling at Beth and Beth apologising. Hope had bled out of Anna's form, leaving her a hollow, bitter womxn. She'd worn her heart on her sleeve and had it stomped underneath Beth's feet, there was nothing to do now, grovelling further would be pathetic and she didn't want Beth to think of her as pathetic.

Anna absentmindedly rubbed her chest. How could her heart hurt so bad? That wasn't scientifically possible, was it?

She needed to get a hold of herself before she did something stupid; like cry.

Eventually, Beth removed the phone from her ear and set it back on the dashboard, she didn't look at Anna. "That was Carrie."

"I guessed." Anna said in a stoic voice. She was holding it together well on the outside, maybe she really was a robot like people liked to say about her.

"I – I don't know what to say, Anna." Beth said. She sighed and wiped away tears from her eyes. "I hate that I have to do this to you, to the both of you."

Anna still managed to keep it together, even though she didn't like being lumped in with Carrie.

"There's no need to say anything to me, Beth."

"I'm so sorry. Carrie has nobody, I'm all she's got and I just can't do that to her, I can't be selfish."

Anna made a sound of agreement, at this point she was out of words, afraid that the next thing she tried to say would come out as a squeaky cry.

"I've got to make this work with Carrie. This whole trip was about her, about saving our relationship and she, even though she's stubborn she wants that too." Beth held up her phone. "That was what this call was about, she wants to come meet us at Margate."

And just when Anna thought it couldn't get any worse, it happened to get very much worse.

She might even be able to handle the rest of the drive to Margate; she might be able to play her part as lawyer in front of the tenants that were waiting for them. She might be able to put up a professional front and smile through it, but having Carrie there? Anna didn't think she could handle that; she didn't think she could be professional in front of that womxn. Anna had never felt so much deep resentment for a person she didn't even know like that. Carrie was the reason that Beth's light was dimmed. She was the reason why Beth second guessed herself with every passing thought and now Anna was going to be forced to be civilised to her?

She made another sound that was a cross between a snort and a cry for help. Beth, thankfully didn't say any more about Carrie.

"We'll be at the house in a few minutes." Anna said. "The visit may not last up to an hour. Will Carrie be able to make it to the house in time?"

Beth clenched her jaw, "We'll stay longer if we have to. The both of us have to make this work."

There was nothing to say to that. Anna revved up the engine and continued driving again.

CHAPTER *FIFTEEN*

The house wasn't much to look at from the outside, it had a nice looking lawn, with a few trees surrounding by the side of it and a small garage with an up and over door. It was modern looking too, not the kind of house that Anna expected to see in a town like Margate.

It was all tall windows. The neighbourhood was nice too, some of the other houses were under renovation and would likely go on to sell for hundreds of thousands. Anna knew that this house was worth almost five hundred thousand pounds, not a bad place to inherit by the looks of it but Beth was staring at it like it caused her a lot of pain.

She remembered Beth's words, about how confronting the house meant that she would have to come to terms with the fact that her aunt was truly gone. An hour ago, Anna would have reached out and held her hand but now, an invisible barrier had been drawn between them, one that she couldn't breach.

It still hurt her that Beth was hurt.

"It's a nice neighbourhood. I can see you enjoying living here." Anna said, a little forcefully. She meant the words though, she was looking at the lawn and thinking how it could easily be converted to a lovely garden that Beth would thrive in. How Beth would come to adore the peace and quiet. Even though she might not know it yet, the house was the best gift she could ever receive in her life.

Beth smiled. "You think so?"

Anna nodded. "I think so."

"I can't believe that I'm finally doing this."

Anna couldn't even bring herself to make a joke about that; she'd never been good at telling jokes in the first place. There was a reason she was speaking too few words; she was afraid that she would cry and beg Beth to choose her again. Apparently, there were no limits to the depths of her pathetic behaviour.

Beth turned to face Anna and her heart broke all over again. As if she needed further proof that Beth was not immune to the pain that was hollowing out Anna's chest. At least Anna managed to keep a mostly stoic face, Beth wore her feelings on her sleeve; her makeup was running down her face and her eyes were bloodshot from crying and there was that bloody horrible skirt. Beth looked like a mess but oddly, she was still as endearing to Anna as she would be if she was wearing the most beautiful clothes.

Anna felt a wave of affection for her. How was it possible to love someone this deeply even though they might never feel the same?

"How do I look?" Beth asked, jolting Anna back to the present. "I don't feel very landlady-ee."

Anna blinked, despite herself; she reached out to wipe Beth's face with the handkerchief she'd kept in the cup holder. Her movements were clinical, her eyes never dwelling on Beth's face as she attempted to make her look presentable. When she was through, she managed to muster up a smile.

"You look great." She declared. It looked like Beth might smile at her, the corner of her lips lifted up in a ghost of a smile before fading away as quickly as it had appeared. Anna was struck with the realisation that the moment the both of them stepped out of the car, then they would cease being Anna and Beth; they would be solicitor and client.

The realisation was the final nail on the coffin, dealing the cruellest blow to Anna. She inhaled sharply and without warning, she opened her door and got out of the car. Best to get this over with as soon as they could.

Together, the two of them quietly climbed the front door steps. Anna gave a sweep of her hand, gesturing that Beth should open the door. Beth cast her a hesitant look that Anna pretended not to see. Beth's habit to allow others to make decisions for her wasn't a good thing, it meant that she never lived life for herself, content to let others do it for her so that she didn't have to live with any feelings of regret. Too bad, Anna was done feeding that toxic habit.

Beth finally knocked and barely three seconds later, they heard the sound of approaching footsteps from inside the house. The tenants hadn't given up on their arrival after all. The door opened wide and a tall elderly womxn wearing a floral print gown opened the door. Anna was struck by how elegantly she looked; the pearl earrings she wore and her blonde hair was mostly white was packed up in a complicated chignon.

"Hello." The womxn said slowly. Anna tried to remember the name she'd been given when she called in the morning.

The womxn looked at them expectantly, there was a certain glint in her eyes that told Anna that she was well aware of who they were, she was pretending not to, wanting them to offer their names first. It was the only sign that Anna needed to know that their presence was not welcome. She had warned Beth that it would be a messy battle if the tenants refused to settle. It was starting to look like that prediction was going to come to pass. Except, Anna wasn't so apathetic anymore, now that she'd seen the house and knew that it was a place that Beth would thrive, she would fight tooth and nail so that Beth got what she deserved in the end, preferably without Carrie but she was going to start with winning over the clients.

Aha, she remembered this womxn's name.

"You're the one I spoke to on the phone earlier." Anna said carefully.

The womxn's answer was a tilt of her head to the right. Anna tried to tamp down on the fizz of irritation rising in her chest, she didn't like discourteous behaviour.

"Nice to meet you, Dr. Susan Parker. I'm Anna Fenwick and this is Elizabeth Granger who is my client and the landlady of this property." Anna said curtly. She gestured from Beth to Dr. Parker hastily. "Now, if we could get on with what we came here for."

Susan Parker looked a little shocked when Beth held out a hand in greeting.

"Hi, Susan, you can call me Beth."

Anna almost giggled hysterically at that moment. Susan had the grace not to let her horror show but Beth did look quite the mess and was being extra friendly on top of. Dr. Parker probably thought she was being pranked. In the end, she took Beth's outstretched hand and gave it a brief shake.

"Nice to meet you. Call me Susan." Was it Anna's imagination or did Dr. Parker sound a little warmer too? Beth seemed to have that effect on most people; she just had the purest of intentions written clearly on her face that it was near impossible to hate her.

"Please, come in." Susan said, opening the door wider so that they could step inside.

Anna was pleasantly surprised by how homey it looked inside the living room. Colourful sofas faced each other with a coffee table in the middle. Deep blue curtains framed the huge windows but they'd been drawn to the ends. Everywhere Anna looked, she saw color; on the art on the walls, on the swirly wallpaper. It looked like a unicorn had thrown up inside the living room but somehow, all the combinations of colours worked.

"It's beautiful in here." Beth said, echoing Anna's thoughts. She took a step forward and stopped, looking bashful as if she didn't own every inch of the house. "So many colours."

With every compliment, Susan seemed to be thawing, an almost grandmotherly smile spread on her face at Beth's words. Something told Anna that Susan wasn't the type of person to hold malicious grudges or be hateful. Perhaps Anna had misjudged her. After all, for all Susan knew, her home was going to be taken away by the big bad Londoner landlady and her awful lawyer. Anna didn't blame her for being defensive at all.

"Thank you, the room was specifically designed to invoke a feeling of warmth and happiness." Susan explained.

Anna quirked her brows. "Really? Does that actually work?"

Susan's smile dimmed a little as she faced Anna. Something seemed to pass on her face but it was gone before Anna could decipher it. "Are you a sceptic, Miss Fenwick?"

"I'm just saying, I don't see how sitting in a room of bright colours will invoke feelings of sunshine and happiness in me." Anna said a little too sarcastically. Susan's smile fell off at the words and Anna immediately found herself regretful. It was too late to take the words back without admitting to Susan that she'd had the worst day ever – scratch that, she'd had the best day ever turn into the worst nightmare.

"Are you a medical doctor, Susan?" Beth asked, cutting into the tension smoothly. Anna was reminded of how Beth had spoken to Brother

Gilbert in the same calm, reassuring manner.

Susan's smile returned. "No, I have my PhD in clinical psychology.

"That's interesting. Are you also a licensed therapist?" Beth asked as they moved further into the house. Susan gestured that they sat down. Anna took the opposite sofa from Beth – Susan frowned at that but she didn't say anything. Anna knew that they should be keeping a united front before the tenants but she couldn't bring herself to care.

Susan sat down beside Anna. "I don't practise anymore. These days, I focus more on research work."

Beth nodded. "That's as important as practising."

Susan beamed back with a smile so bright that it took Anna aback. She nodded several enthusiastic times. "Exactly what I tell people, most people just don't get it. It's the important research that gives way to better treatment methods and leads to important discovery that changes the way mental health is perceived."

"I wanted to work in research after graduation too." Beth said. This, Anna didn't know, Beth hadn't mentioned that to her and she couldn't help but recall Beth's argument that Anna didn't really know her.

"I didn't know that." Anna said, her voice a little accusing. Two pairs of eyes turned to her, both of them baffled.

"Oh, I don't think I ever told you that." Beth answered carefully, she was looking at Anna a little wearily, as if she was a ticking bomb that might explode any moment and make a mess everywhere.

"That explains it." Anna said in a clipped tone and went back to saying nothing.

"Dear, what did you study?" Susan asked, no doubt trying to chase away all the lingering awkwardness and she'd appeared to take a liking to Beth. Good, that would make it easier to convince her to settle.

"I majored in Plant Biology and a minor in Business Administration." Beth said. "I always dreamed of being surrounded by plants and during important research work but it didn't happen that way."

"Oh, well, I just know that you'd love what the ladies have done with the back garden, it's no fancy greenhouse but it is absolutely beautiful."

Susan said enthusiastically.

"The lawn looks great, I really like what you've done with the place and I would definitely love to see the back garden." Beth said but there was barely any enthusiasm in her voice, the cheer was mostly forced but Susan didn't seem to notice, she just seemed glad that she had found common ground with Beth.

Anna was left confused for a second. Did Beth not love the house? Was she having a change of mind?

"Where are my manners? Is there anything I could get you to drink? There's tea and Nancy makes lemonade fresh if you prefer something more cooling." Susan asked.

"I'm good, thank you." Anna answered briskly.

Susan turned hopeful eyes to Beth. She couldn't have looked more desperate if she tried. Anna could sense Beth's hesitance wavering and found herself a little annoyed. Would it kill Beth to say no to something she didn't want for once? Everybody else's feelings be damned.

"I'll have some lemonade." She finally answered.

Susan leapt to her feet with surprising agility. "Wonderful, I'll go get you a glass and you'll meet the rest of everybody. Just wait right here for me." She added.

Rest of who?

"Wait a second, how many people live here?" Anna blurted. Susan halted in her step, throwing a careless answer over her shoulder. "Oh, it's just the five of us. And there's Jane Doe."

She was gone before Anna could ask her to expand on that. There was awkward silence when she was gone. Beth glanced around the living room with unashamed curiosity while Anna tried to stare at anything but Beth. She hoped that Susan returned quickly with the lemonade because Anna didn't know how long she could keep on the charade of nonchalance.

***

Simon was awake and just like Susan had predicted, he was different. There was a bright flush to his cheeks, a twinkling joy in his eyes that was a little scary because of how genuine it looked. He was happy, to put it lightly, maybe more than happy, try ecstatic. He'd already hugged Felicity seven times and was greeting Hunter effusively as if he hadn't seen him in years.

He'd even hugged Susan too when she'd walked into the room. She'd been both surprised by the hug and the fact that he was awake.

"I heard someone trying to open the door and found him awake, it's strange, isn't it?" Hunter had said when Susan asked who'd first found him.

Susan felt a little cold, knowing how close Simon had been to coming into the living room and finding Elizabeth Granger and Anna Fenwick. His behaviour would have been downright scary to them but not to Susan who had anticipated his changed but erratic behaviour. The trip was supposed to change people, their outlook on life and mortality and Simon had woken up with a renewed view of his life. Right now, as Susan took his vitals, he was openly sobbing, crying unabashedly and talking about how he'd taken life for granted and how he was never going to do that again.

The rest were looking at him a little strangely, there was no missing the happiness on their faces but they found it hard reconciling the Simon before the psychedelic trip to this Simon.

"This is so strange. It's like he's high." Hunter said, crossing meaty arms over another and shaking his head as he looked at Simon. Normally, Susan didn't like to allow all of them into the room at once for a fear that their presence would tamper with the experiment somehow. But Simon was awake now and for all their eyes to see.

"Is he supposed to be this happy?" Felicity asked, but she didn't sound worried at all. She was smiling big, ear to ear. She more than anybody knew who Simon was the most. The rest of them had known Simon in his worst state, miserable and tired of life. Only Felicity had seen a different kind of Simon.

"It's an elevated state of mind now. He's bound to be like this for a few hours." Susan answered, she finished listening to Simon's heartbeat and took the stethoscope away. "His heart rate is a little higher than normal but it isn't anything to worry about. I'd advise just keeping an eye on him and maybe bringing him some food."

"Food, I took advantage of something so simple before." Simon said from where he was seated, his eyes slightly glazed over, no doubt thinking of what he'd eat. Or rather, the simple pleasure of eating.

"This is such a huge problem right now." Nancy said. "We're going to have to keep him hidden and it was already hard doing so while he was asleep, now we're going to have to do it with a hyperactive Simon?"

"We have to keep him out of sight and in this room at all costs. His inhibitions are low so his behavior will be erratic and strange." Susan explained. "Any ideas?"

"We'll say that this room and your office have been varnished and that we have to keep the doors closed so that the fumes can leave through the window." Hunter said quickly. "And we can lock Simon inside the room."

Susan winced visibly. "I don't think we can do that. Simon's emotions are at an all high, locking him and preventing his freedom may turn his emotions negative."

Felicity's smile became a frown. "That can happen?" She asked.

"It's plausible." Susan said. She turned to Simon and adopted a stern expression on her face. "Simon, are you listening to me?" She asked.

His wild eyes turned to her, not quite focusing on her face but roaming everywhere, alight with wonder as if he hadn't seen any of these things before. "Dr. Parker, you saved my life." His words were slightly slurred. Hunter was right, it did seem as if he was high.

"Yes, so you have to listen to me very carefully." She began. "You have to stay in here and not come out. Felicity will bring you something to eat but you have to stay here. Look outside the window; meditate on the wonders outside of this window. But you can't leave this room, you aren't ready yet." She spoke in calm, careful words, the way one might speak to a child. He seemed to be paying attention to her though as she spoke.

"No going outside." He repeated her words.

She gave him a smile and a nod. "Good." She turned to the rest of them. "Hunter, you'll keep coming back here to check on him but right now, we all have to meet the landlady."

***

It was getting unbearable sitting so close to Beth yet feeling at the same time like she was so far away. By now, Anna had given up on the charade of pretending like she didn't care. She cared very much, she cared that Beth was about to make the biggest mistake of her life and she didn't even know it.

The urge to voice these concerns out loud were almost suffocating, threatening to pour from her tongue in hot, scalding words. Because she was getting tired of the vague hints, the truth needed to be shaken in Beth's face, devoid of any misconceptions.

Just when she thought she might actually do it, Susan returned with a tray of Beth's lemonade and a bunch of other people in tow. A pregnant womxn and a burly man that Anna assumed was her husband, judging by the way he stood protectively by her side. There was another womxn and Anna almost missed the small swell of her stomach.

Susan set the tray down before Beth with a smile and clapped her hands together. "These are the rest of the family. Meet Hunter," she gestured to the man. "Nancy and Felicity."

"I'm Elizabeth Granger, but you can call me Beth. And this is Anna Fenwick, my lawyer."

The title was a slap in Anna's face. It was hard to keep the hurt off her face, harder to keep acting indifferent. She longed to jump out of her own skin but she'd settle for not sitting in the same room with Beth and pretend like she was nothing but the legal help.

The other tenants muttered greetings but it was Nancy who struck Anna as defiant, she made no attempt to hide the open look of disdain on her face.

"Nice to meet all of you." Beth said, still trying to keep the peace. "This place looks wonderful."

Her cheer was met with silence and her smile wavered just a little bit. Anna kept waiting, for Beth's eyes to meet hers, for reassurance or guidance. It seemed to her that Beth was avoiding her too. It made Anna's hackles rise up even more, was it that easy for Beth to pretend?

She was so lost in her thoughts that she missed part of the conversation. She blinked to Beth standing up and everybody looking at her expectantly.

"Are you alright, Miss Fenwick? You look a little green." Susan asked in genuine concern. Anna stiffened.

"I'm fine." She stood up, assuming they were about to be given a tour of the house. She hoped it was a quick one. She, after all, still had a job to complete here.

And to think that they were doing this for Carrie. Keeping away from each other because Beth felt a sense of duty and obligation to that womxn.

Susan was engaging Beth in small talk, about the weather and how London was like — apparently, she hadn't been to the city in almost a decade.

"I've discovered that coastal town suit me more than any cities would. There's just an inner peace that small towns bring, along with a sense of neighbourhood and belonging." Susan said as they entered the door on the left, it was the kitchen.

It was bigger than Anna expected. Spacious too, there was a small dining setting facing the window — three antique looking chairs that matched an equally antique looking table, the furniture looked like something that belonged in an auction.

"I can agree with that." Beth said. "We got lost during our drive here and met the Unvaredonia community. Have you heard of them?"

Susan nodded. "Ah, they're quite reclusive."

Beth gave a little shrug as she came to stand near the dining table. Anna immediately moved to the other end of the kitchen, pretending as if she was marvelled by the kitchenware.

"But their way of life is charming, to let go of all worldly attachment and choose to lead a simple life is interesting to say the least." Beth explained.

The other tenants looked as awkward as Anna must feel on the inside. It was as if they were waiting for the other shoe to drop and chaos to ensue. The pregnant womxn — Nancy — kept shooting daggers at Anna. If it was up to her, Anna and Beth would have never been allowed into the house. Anna frowned, wondering what misconceptions that Nancy had of them in her head.

Beth wandered to the window, looking outside. She turned to Susan and grinned, "I love the view."

"Well, so do we." Nancy cut in tartly.

Awkward silence ensued. Susan shot Nancy a warning look but Anna wasn't sure that the message was succinctly received. Nancy's frown didn't waver for once.

Susan coughed, trying to regain control of the situation. "Let's look at the back garden. You'd love it, Beth."

"Yes." The other womxn, Felicity, said quickly. "The garden is very lovely. Right this way."

Felicity immediately hurried for the door and ushered all of them out of the kitchen.

Susan and Anna hung back, leisurely in their pace while Felicity chatted up a storm with Beth about a flytrap or something. The burly man, Hunter was whispering something to his wife, his eyes darting up for a brief second, communicating a message that Anna didn't understand. Her thoughts were too scattered to try and decipher it either. She was here to get a job done and that was it — or so she thought.

***

The garden was beautiful, a burst of several colours that had her looking around, wanting to take in all the sights at once.

"Wow, there's a bit of everything in here." Beth said. She got the sense that the other tenants didn't appreciate their presence and if she was being honest, they were right to be worried. This wasn't a friendly visit, she was going to take their home from them and move in with Carrie. Somehow, the thought didn't excite her like it had a few days ago. She was so close to getting everything she wanted; the house and the girl, yet she ominously felt like she was making the wrong choice.

Beth didn't know how it had hurt her to pick Carrie, to do the right thing. She remembered something that her aunt used to say; about how the right people came at the wrong time. Her aunt had never been married and Beth wondered if she had fallen in love with someone she couldn't have.

"Yes, at first I started with the lavenders." It was Felicity who was kind enough to talk to her. The others just stared at her. She pointed at a patch of lavenders, as if Beth could have missed their purple brilliance. "And then the herbs and random other bits."

"You did this all by yourself?" Beth asked, awe in her voice.

Felicity gave a humble shrug. "I had help, Nancy helps out."

"This is all your work, Felicity." Nancy said but she somehow managed to make the words sound like a jab at Beth.

Felicity ignored Nancy. "Plus I have too much time on my hands. You're something of a green thumb too?"

Beth smiled halfheartedly. "I suppose. I studied plants at university."

"That's amazing. What do you do now, lab work or research?" The interest in felicity's voice was genuine too.

"No, I work in real estate."

Beth could see that it wasn't the answer that Felicity had been expecting. How did one go from studying plant biology to working in real estate? It was so sad that Beth wanted to laugh. How did she end up doing everything but the things that she wanted to do?

"That's interesting." Felicity managed because she was nice.

"It's really not. I'm not complaining that it's a bad job by any means but it definitely isn't what I wanted to do. Anyways, in my place back in London I have a hothouse where I take care of carnivorous plants – I have a soft spot for misunderstood things." Beth said.

Felicity's eyes lit up. "Wow, granted I don't know much about carnivorous plants but it must take a lot to be able to breed them."

Beth laughed, feeling a little lighter than she had all afternoon. "They are pretty demanding things, I won't lie."

"So you have commitments in the city, Miss Granger?" Nancy asked. Beth regarded her warily, certain that she was walking into a trap.

"Yes. I have a girlfriend and--" She almost let it out that she and Carrie were planning to move to Margate. "And there's my job but I mostly work from home anyways."

Nancy made a noncommittal hum. "Well, the statistics say that city people always hate it in the suburbs, it's one of the leading causes of depression in the suburbs."

Beth gave her a puzzled smile. "Okay, thank you for telling me."

"It's illegal to evict tenants out of a house without the proper warning given." Nancy continued.

"Nancy!" Felicity whisper-shouted.

Beth felt the onset of a headache. "It's fine, thank you for letting me know." She muttered distractedly. She allowed herself to look behind, inside the house where Anna and Susan were discussing with serious looks on their faces. She felt a sharp pain in her chest at the sight of Anna. Never had Beth wanted to be selfish her whole life, to seize something she wanted so desperately to her chest.

But what about Carrie? Her mind asked. Carrie who wasn't perfect by any means, who was cold and mean to Beth, Carrie who had nobody on her side but Beth. No matter how desperately Beth might want Anna, she couldn't find it in herself to sever all ties with Carrie.

Or perhaps, it's because she's your safety net, the other part of her mind taunted. Carrie lived life for the both of them that Beth felt she didn't have to lift a finger; she had the nice paying job, the approval of her parents and the perfect sociable girlfriend. Except none of those things brought the satisfaction that Beth thought they would bring and the thought of confronting the fact that she was deeply unhappy in life and her relationship was unsettling.

Here she was, planning to kick out these people from their pleasures life; ready to move in because she thought that it would fix the rift in her relationship yet she was not willing to confront why that rift existed in the first place.

Distantly, she heard Felicity talking about the trees and how they provided excellent shade for the strawberries.

"I think I've seen enough." Beth declared abruptly.

Felicity's face fell. Beth felt sorry that she was being curt with the only person making the effort to know her but she was so conflicted with her feelings that her head spun. Even though she was acting contrary, she did love the house and she could imagine herself living here, but somehow, the image of living here with Carrie had slowly begun to bleed out of the whole picture. It was Anna's face that Beth saw when she closed her eyes.

"Are you okay, Beth?" Felicity was asking.

"Yes, sorry, I just think we should continue with the rest of the tour." She added.

"Alright, as you wish." Felicity said, smiling a hurt smile.

Beth would find a way to make it up to her later, perhaps she'd end up not living here after all.

***

Susan and Anna hung back as everybody else piled into the back garden through a sliding door. From where she stood, she could see that the garden was bigger than she'd thought. She was used to back gardens being much smaller. When she'd been younger, it had been a little hobby of her father's to tend to the lawn at the back of their house, he'd mow it and keep the grass trim and nice. It was only when Anna was older that she realised that her mother had been pregnant and that the baby had been a boy. She'd had a miscarriage four months into being pregnant though. Back then, her father had been keeping the grass nice so he could kick a ball around with his son. He'd even installed small goalposts and everything.

After her mother lost the baby, he'd stopped mowing it as often. Sometimes, he'd let the grass grow tall and wild.

This one was nothing like Anna's garden though, it was bigger and more beautiful, filled with green plants and what looked like a few flowers. Beth would thrive here. She imagined her tending to the plants, wearing a sundress and a straw hat, a warm smile on her face as she tilted her head towards the sun — soaking in the sunlight. Anna's imagination soon turned sour when she visualised Carrie coming into the garden to wrap her arms around Beth.

In this daydream, Carrie was shooting Anna a smug smile and mouthing the words, "I win."

Anna clenched her fists, she'd never particularly had violent tendencies until now. She was going to drag Carrie by her smug hair and shake her until she was blue in the face.

"What are your intentions with this place?" Susan asked, her voice snapping Anna back to the present.

Anna blinked, surprised by the suddenness of the question. She'd thought that they would get all the pleasantries and tour out of the way before they got down to discussing business. It seemed that Susan had other ideas though.

"My intentions?" She echoed in confusion. "I'm a property solicitor, Dr. Parker and I represent Miss Granger. It's not about my intention, I'm here to offer my services — not only to her, but concerning the recently inherited house."

Susan frowned but she didn't say anything at first. "How long have you been a solicitor?"

Anna was genuinely taken aback by the question. "I beg your pardon. I don't see how relevant that is—"

"You just seem so young." Susan added softly. "You remind me a little of my daughter."

Anna stiffened; she'd never reminded anyone of family before. Most people usually thought that she was odd. But Anna wasn't like Beth. Beth would smile and say something appropriate for the situation. Beth had easily won over Susan while she still regarded Anna with suspicion.

"Long enough." Anna answered firmly. Even though Susan's question had seemed harmless. To soften the blow of her stiff words, she added, "How many children do you have?"

It was Susan's turn to stiffen. She attempted a smile but there was something sad about it. "I have two children."

Anna nodded, her instinct told her not to pry further into that question. She didn't want to say the wrong thing. "So these people, they aren't exactly your family."

That too was apparently the wrong thing to say because Susan shot her a mild look. "Family isn't always blood. They're family to me in the ways that count."

Anna didn't understand that, sure, she'd heard of people referring to their best friends as like family but she'd never been able to relate. She guessed that it didn't matter after all. "And how long have you all lived here?" Anna asked; she was beginning to sound like a lawyer now.

"Is this an interrogation? Should I have my own lawyer present?" Susan's words sounded jocular enough but there was an underlying layer of tension in her voice. Anna understood that she was trying to ask their true intentions for the house. But the truth was that Anna wasn't even sure. She and Beth weren't exactly on communicating terms right now — both as lawyer and client and as friends? Lovers?

"Don't be ridiculous." Anna said, trying to make her voice sound light and jocular as Susan's words. Part of being a lawyer was knowing how to appease the good sides of people, to get them to see you as their best friends. Anna had never tried to play that game before. It wasn't her style, she'd rather get straight to the point and be frank about it.

Good thing she was a quick study when it came to learning new things.
"We've lived here for the better part of a year." Susan finally answered.

"Did you know the previous landlady?" Anna asked.

Susan's answer was a shake of her head. "I got the house through an agent, there was never any need for direct contact between the both of us. And I've never had any problems with the house that I'd have to contact her."

"Hmm." Anna hummed noncommittally. She'd learnt that people offered more information when they were subtly prompted. A gentle nudge was all she needed to get them to talk.

Although Susan was a psychologist. Did that mean she was immune to such a tactic?

"However, a lawyer reached out a few months ago to let us know that the ownership had changed and that the old landlady died."

"How did you feel about that?" Anna asked.

Susan was visibly taken aback by the question. She laughed but it was more shocking than amusing. "Goodness, how was I supposed to feel? I suppose I was shocked and I waited a while for the new landlady to get in touch so I could offer my condolences but she never did."

Anna felt defensive on Beth's behalf despite everything. "She was grieving. The previous landlady had been her aunt, a womxn that she was deeply close with. The house wasn't on her list of priorities."

"And now?" Susan boldly asked.

Anna was saved from answering the question when Beth and the others returned from the garden. She didn't look happy like Anna had expected she would stepping into the garden. Instead, she was worrying her bottom lip excessively and averting her gaze from Anna's.

"Did you like the garden?" Susan asked immediately.
"Marvellous, it was beautiful." Beth said but her words lacked any cheer, she sounded as if she was repeating words that had been spoken to her.

Susan seemed to sense that, she hesitated and cast Anna a questioning look that she pretended not to see.

Anna clapped her hands together a little too enthusiastically. "Great, let's carry on with the tour, shall we?"

And so they did, Susan led them to the stairs that led to the second floor. She talked about how the house was an art deco built in 1930 and how she'd tried to maintain antique and modern aesthetics as in the kitchen and the furniture in the living room. Anna was only half listening.

"There are four bedrooms, three bathrooms, and an office space," Susan added offhandedly.

"Wait, did you say office space?" Anna asked.

Susan's smile wavered. "Yes."

"Can we see that?" Anna asked. Her own home didn't have a study which was one of the reasons she stayed late past closing hours at the firm if she wanted to get ahead of work.

She thought it might be something Beth would like in a house, knowing that she worked in real estate and not knowing whether she planned to abandon the family business full time when she moved to Margate.

"My own home doesn't come with its office. I'm left working overtime at the firm if I want to get some extra work done." Anna explained. Nobody laughed or said that they could relate.

Anna felt her cheeks heat up in embarrassment.

"Er, that won't be possible." Susan said with what was supposed to be an apologetic smile, it looked more like a grimace though.

Anna's sham of a smile fell. "Why not?"

"We varnished the house recently." Felicity answered. "One of the rooms and Susan's office. We've kept the doors locked so that the fumes go out through the windows instead." She made a face. "You have to tell us about your job, what do solicitors do?" She asked.

Susan looked like she would expire in relief at Felicity's interruption and Anna frowned.

"Yes, you have to tell us. I can't keep up with all these lawyer terms. What's the difference between a regular lawyer and a solicitor?" Hunter asked, this was the first time he was speaking a single word to Anna.

"Well, lawyer is the umbrella term. A solicitor is a type of lawyer whose traditional role is to offer legal services to clients apart from acting as their advocate in court." Anna explained briskly.

"Wow, fascinating." Susan said in a pitchy voice. Why did she sound nervous all of a sudden?

Before Anna could question her on it, she was opening the door to one of the bedrooms. She left the door wide open and gestured for them to step in. The others, who likely used one of these bedrooms, allowed them to go through first.

The bedroom was less eccentric compared to the rest of the house that they'd seen so far; white walls, king-sized bed and an en-suite bathroom. The first thing that Anna noticed was the tabby cat on the made bed. She startled at the sight of it.

Susan laughed. "That's Jane Doe."

"She's a stray. She kept coming into the house and leaving so we started leaving food for her so she would stop by often." Felicity said, with genuine fondness in her voice.

"Aw, what a gorgeous kitty." Beth cooed, she went over to the cat to rub her ears. Surprisingly, the creature was friendly, leaning into Beth's hand. Anna found herself jealous of the cat.

Another picture fit into her mind like the end piece of a puzzle. Of course Jane Doe got to be a part of Beth's life but Anna wouldn't.

"She's not a kitty." Nancy pointed out a matter of factly.

Beth ignored her and continued petting the cat, a light that hadn't been there before entering into her eyes.

Beth looked up, meeting Anna's eyes for the first time in the past hour. "I'm not really an animal person but I like her." She said hesitantly, as if she wanted to adopt her but asking her partner's opinion.

Anna felt warms; she wasn't losing Beth. Not yet. For the longest moment, silence stretched out like a suffocating blanket until it choked Anna; she didn't know what to say. She felt exposed. The cat was meowing, annoyed to no longer be the subject of Beth's attention.

Susan continued talking about the house without missing a beat and moved on to the other bedroom. She was regaling a distracted Beth about the large roof terrace with sea views.

Anna slipped away from them quietly, thinking that she might go back downstairs to get some air. She walked past the room that Susan claimed had been varnished, pausing curiously in her steps. Her hand reached for the knob and she twisted it open, wincing when the door made a creaking sound.

CHAPTER *SIXTEEN*

The room was white. White curtains drawn over the windows that stood still as if there was no air in the room, white fluorescent lights overhead. The walls painted a blinding shade of white too, matching the sheets on the bed and the man sitting on the white sofa, receiving medicine from a standing drip. Anna blinked and almost missed him.

She let out a little scream of fright when she noticed the man wearing a white t-shirt and sweatpants and looking pale. His hair was a shaggy brown that looked as if he just rolled out of bed – she might have thought so too if the bed wasn't freshly made.

"Who are you?" Anna asked. Or more importantly, what kind of freakish nightmare has she stumbled into?

The man in the chair blinked slowly at her, taking in her form. She was taken aback when his lips stretched into a smile, wide and genuine. Anna could have sworn that she'd never met this man in her life before but she was beginning to doubt herself now, nobody smiled at random strangers like that; that beam was reserved for loved ones.

"Ah, you must be the reason why I wasn't allowed to come downstairs." The man said. He shook his head and Anna was surprised when he stood up and began to approach her in slow steps, the medical drip was on tiny wheels that he dragged along with him as he walked. Anna stood, rooted to the spot, feeling a mixture of fright and curiosity. Her gut feeling about Susan's caginess had been right; she and the rest of the tenants had lied about the room being varnished. They'd been hiding this man.

The man held out his free hand to Anna. "I'm Simon." His smile was back, free and unhinged. Anna was starting to get a little scared of it. She stared at his extended hand as if he was handing her a bloody, severed arm instead. Her eyes roamed his form, taking in the drugs again.

"What the fuck is going on here? Have they held you against your will? I can call the police." Anna offered, so far this man seemed harmless – save his creepy smile -- but the moment Anna mentioned the police, pure unadulterated fear entered his eyes.

"You can't!" He exclaimed, loudly. Anna winced, fearing her eardrums would explode. There was a chill in the room that reminded her of being in a freezer. Was this Susan's doing? Why was she keeping this man behind these doors? And what was with the drugs?

"Dr. Parker is helping me."

Anna recoiled from him, taking a step back. What kind of sci-fi hell had she stepped into?

The door opened behind her and Susan stepped in, wearing a look of absolute horror on her face. "Anna." She breathed out, gaping as she tried to find the next words to say.

The man on the other hand looked excited to see Susan, he staggered towards her and embraced her in a hug that she didn't flinch from, her arms hanging limply by her side, resigned to the hug. The sight was almost comical to Anna and she was pretty sure that she would soon go into hysteria if she didn't get an explanation very soon.

"Dr. Parker, I'm so happy to see you." And he meant it too, his voice muffled as he tucked his chin into the crook of Susan's shoulder. He pulled out of the hug a second later. "I met your friend." He gestured one hand at Anna with the same enthusiasm. "I was telling her about how your experiment changed my life."

Anna's mind began to wander, it seemed to her that Susan was carrying out something weird in here and from the whole secrecy, Anna was willing to bet that it wasn't legal. But was it dangerous? That she didn't know here. Simon's cheeks were flushed with life and he was breaking into a grin every few seconds but he seemed fine? He reminded Anna of someone who was high on drugs. She once got surgery for her appendix removal and afterwards, she'd been in such pain that they'd had to put her on morphine, maybe a little too much because she'd kept smiling idiotically. Simon reminded her of that.

"What is going on here, Susan?" Anna asked, trying to make her voice stern but failing, she was mostly curious.

Susan sighed and gently led Simon back to the sofa. "Sit," She told him and he obeyed.

"The cat's out of the bag it seems." Susan said with a resigned look.

Anna felt a pang of sympathy towards her, now that the secret was out, Susan didn't have to keep up a front anymore, she suddenly looked exhausted, the bags under her eyes visible as she rubbed them.

"The cat is me." Simon piped up from behind Susan.

Anna couldn't tamp down on her smile fast enough, it burst free and Susan noticed it.

She chuckled. "He wasn't like this before but this is a much more welcome state of mind than before."

"This isn't legal, is it?" Anna asked. The solicitor in her was spinning, if Susan was found out to be conducting illegal research then Anna could blackmail her to leave the house if she didn't want to be arrested.

But Susan would be in trouble and who knew how much; it would be a shame too because Anna actually liked her. Such a strange day, first she'd fallen for a womxn she'd never known prior to today and now she found herself liking a bunch of strangers.

"No, it's not," Susan said, she lifted a defiant chin. "But I'm not ashamed of my work."

"Are you even a clinical psychologist? Or is that code for a mad scientist?" Anna couldn't help but ask.

Now Susan just looked offended. "Of course I'm a psychologist. I have my Master's and PhD in Clinical Psychology. Want me to show you my certificates?"

"In the office that was allegedly varnished?" Anna shot back. Guilt flashed in Susan's eyes and Anna felt bad immediately. It was clear that Susan hadn't enjoyed lying to them. "I'm sorry."

Susan sighed. "I don't blame you, at least you haven't run out and scream for the police yet."

Anna frowned. "That's mostly because I still don't get the full picture of what is going on here."

"Please, enlighten me," Anna added politely.

"What you're looking at is my life's work, what was supposed to be my magnum opus. I planned to change the way mental illness is treated." Susan began. She walked to the made bed and sat down at the edge. Anna thought of joining her and sitting down but she preferred to be closer to the door where it was easier if she decided to sprint out of the room and call the police after all. Even though Simon was silent now, his eyes continued to bounce from Susan to Anna, his gaze always straying and never staying. It deeply unsettled Anna and she suspected that she might continue to remain unsettled until whatever was going on was explained to her.

Susan shrugged as if to say, suit yourself.

"I told you that I have two children."

Anna nodded, unsure where Susan was going with the story.

Susan inhaled a deep breath, her voice shook with her next words, "My son took his life on the eve of his thirtieth birthday."

"Oh, I'm so sorry for your loss, Susan." Anna said hurriedly, so that explained the weird sadness that Susan had gotten in her eyes earlier when she mentioned that she had children.

"It was a long time ago." Susan said, waving off the condolence.

"But it's so obviously affected you and even influenced your work. It's okay not to be over it, dare I say that you may never get over it – that too is okay. Grief doesn't get better with time; it just gets different." Anna said matter of factly.

"Susan looked a little surprised at Anna's vehement declaration. "You're right. I assume you've had experience in the grieving department."

"My mother died a couple of years ago. I still miss her every day." Anna admitted.

"I'm sorry for your loss." Susan echoed Anna's earlier words.

"Thank you."

"Anyways, my son had been fighting depression for years before he lost that battle. He was secretive with his struggles and he tried therapy, nothing seemed to be helping. As a therapist, I was exposed to the struggles of other people and to an extent you have to dissociate from it or your own mental health suffers too. But watching your own loved ones go through that struggle and you're unable to help, it breaks something inside of you." Susan explained, her eyes taking on a distant look. Anna saw years of pain in the depths of her eyes.

"After he died, I poured myself into research – I quit being a therapist. I conducted research on the most effective treatment methods. I found myself most fascinated by the idea of creating a drug that would cause the patient to go into an uninterrupted state where they relived their memories without much interference from the outside world – with only the occasional guidance from a psychologist."

Susan gestured to Simon, "He was severely depressed prior to this experiment but look at him now. The drug which is a harmless hallucinogen causes this effect and puts the patient into a sleep-like state. It grants insight to the patient; reveals your own truest heart desires before the brain on the situation."

"Simon has gained insight and is just freshly awake – which explains his erratic energy, I think I may have given him a higher dose of the drug more than needed." She caught Anna's quizzical look and quickly added, "But there are no dangerous side effects."

"He's found joy in the most basic experiences, this is what I wanted to achieve with my work."

Susan was looking at her expectantly and with a mix of fear and hope. Anna knew that for Susan to conduct the experiment without other people knowing, then she'd had to go through plenty of rejections. Maybe some of them were valid or maybe they came from a place of fear too; all that Anna knew was that Simon had been willingly part of the experiment judging by how he'd expressed his appreciations for her help.

"It sounds caring, what you're doing. And it's helping people – or at least someone from the looks of things." Anna finally said, choosing her words carefully.

Susan relaxed visibly. "Thank you."

Anna had one more question though, "How do you know that the effects are permanent? What if this is just a temporary high?"

Susan seemed to carefully consider the question before speaking. "The purpose of the experiment is to assist self-realisation and actualization. He's not going to be like this forever, in fact, this effect is bound to wear off in the next few hours. He'll be calmer, much more confident in himself because of what he visualised during the experiment."

"If I'm being honest, I'm a little jealous. A drug and experiment that helps you resolve your inner tug of war; I could use some of it right now." Anna punctuated her words with a laugh but she was barely joking. "Something that tells me what I want sounds divine."

Maybe it was the feeling in her voice as she said the words that caused Susan's face to soften.

"There's something bothering you, isn't there?" Susan asked.

Anna didn't even bother to force a laugh this time. "Yes, there is. I'm pretty sure you've pieced together the details, I'm very obvious and you're obviously smart."

Susan's cheeks pinkened at the compliment. She smiled. "It has something to do with a certain blonde hair blue eyed womxn currently seeing the rest of the house without you."

Anna's shoulder slumped. Safety be damned, she crossed the distance to sit on the bed beside Susan. "What gave me away?" She asked sardonically.

"I think I'm in love with her." Anna admitted. "I'm torn to pieces about it because I don't know what to do before it's late."

Having bottled up her feelings, it made Anna feel lighter as she poured them out to Susan.

"She's got a girlfriend, a womxn who doesn't appreciate her the way she deserves to be but Beth doesn't see her – she has this twisted sense of loyalty towards her even though it's killing her." Anna explained. "She doesn't want to hurt her and by extension, I don't want to hurt Beth. I don't want her to choose me and regret it every day for the rest of her life. That is if she even wants to pick me." Anna breathed out, she looked away from Susan's face, unable to handle the sympathy in them. Already she felt the pressure of tears burning against her vision, if she looked at Susan, she might unravel and cry.

Susan stood up and Anna thought she might leave the room, instead she walked to the nightstand on the right side of the bed and opened one of the drawers. She returned back to Anna's side, holding out a round disk like container, she flipped open the lid, revealing the tincture.

"Choose to be happy. Go ahead, I'll guide you."

Anna hesitated, but then she thought of doing nothing and living with this hesitance, this uncertainty and the regret that she could have done something about it – that thought alone was enough to spur her into action. She reached out and took the tincture from Susan.

***

Anna was nowhere to be found, as was Susan. By all the deductions, it seemed as if the both of them were together, perhaps talking about the house, Anna would likely be telling Susan the real reason for their visit. If Anna got Susan to agree to settling, then the others would concede. The thought didn't fill Beth with any kind of consolation, instead she felt quite terrible, sick to her stomach even and she was still wearing the hideous skirt.

She was filled with the sudden desire to see Anna; she was worried about her. Maybe she was in the back garden with Susan. Beth allowed herself to be led back downstairs. Felicity and Hunter made excuses to check on something and they left Beth alone with the heavily pregnant womxn in the living room. Beth walked to the front door, peeking outside to see if Anna and Susan were there; there was nobody in the front garden.

"What really are your intentions for coming here?" Nancy said.

Beth turned to her, baffled by the question. "I don't understand you."

Nancy scoffed. "I think you do, perfectly. You may have everyone fooled with your innocent outlook but I'm on to your game. Everybody knows that rent-collectors are the villains."

Beth almost laughed at that because it sounded like something Carrie would say – scratch that, Carrie did say that a lot.

"My girlfriend likes to say that too." Beth said distractedly, she was patting down the skirt, hearing herself saying, "My girlfriend!"

Where was Anna?

"Well, your girlfriend has a point then." Nancy spat, unrelenting with the jabs. "You can't just kick us out on the streets. The law requires that you give months of notice and we don't owe rent – we're entitled to live here for as long as our rent is valid."

Beth whirled around to face her and laughed in exasperation. She wasn't thinking about the house now; she was thinking that she was making the biggest mistake by letting Anna go. How many people could say that they found their soul mates? How many people could say that they'd developed the most meaningful bond of their lives in less than one day?

But there was Carrie. Beth couldn't let go of that either.

"I'm familiar with the law, I assure you, my family has been doing this for decades." She said dismissively.

"Why do you keep looking out the window?" Nancy's frustrated voice came again.

"If you'd asked me these questions a few days ago, then you would have gotten a much different answer. I never wanted this place in the first place, getting that call from the lawyer months ago that my aunt left me a property and felt like accepting her death. So I ignored it. If I didn't acknowledge it then my aunt was still alive, maybe just far away, I could pretend like she travelled abroad. But my relationship is going to hell, my girlfriend is giving me a fucking hard time and I'm just so…" Beth raked a hand through her hair, it was the first time she was letting herself acknowledge and feel the months, if not years of frustration that Carrie had been putting her through.

"I'm just so fucking sick of it. So I think, maybe moving to some place quieter will help our relationship, maybe we'll get along with each other and stop fighting. I've been begging and pleading and bribing her just so she'd agree to us moving."

Beth stopped mid pace and gave a sudden snort. "She'd probably like you guys, this whole house is so eccentric and artsy that she'd just love it. If she wasn't being an arse about it, an arse is even a nicer word to describe her. The perfect description is a fucking nightmare, that's what she's been. She bullies me, plays the victim if I demand one iota of affection; she tolerates me like one would do to a child. I just try to love her and love her and hope I love her bad parts away but that isn't working."

"A delight, am I right?" She laughed at her own rhyme. "I don't know why I keep doing this. I haven't loved her in a while, I'm only with her because of guilt, nothing ties us together but my own guilt."

Beth paused in her steps, realising two things at once; one that she'd frightened Nancy, the poor womxn was looking at Beth as if she was deranged and two, that every word she'd spoken was the truth. She'd managed to pour out her feelings in one go.

How had it taken her so long to articulate her feelings?

***

Anna felt chills overtake her body; like tiny pin pricks on every pore on her skin. She shivered or at least, she imagined that that was what she did. Her eyes rolled to the back of her head. She was feeling a mix of euphoria and something else, something she couldn't put a finger on.

"Focus on the details, on the sound of my voice, on the emotion bubbling to the surface. Are you warm or cold?" Susan asked.

Anna struggled to hold on to that focus. "Yes, so--" her voice broke off. "So cold." She heard the sound of rattling and realised moments later that it was her teeth making the clattering sound.

"Cold signifies fear. You're afraid, yes?" Susan asked. "What are you afraid of?"

"I'm afraid of making the wrong decision." Anna answered, her voice sounded soft and gentle.

"Focus, Anna, focus."

"—early stage of insight, you've cut all bounds of inhibition. Focus on what your spirit is saying."

"I don't want to lose Beth; I don't want her to live sad for the rest of her life." It was her deepest fear. Anna didn't fear a lot of things, not death, not anything else. She hadn't made a lot of memorable decisions in her lifetime until now. It was the battle of losing love.

She waited for Susan's voice to cut in and tell her what to do and how to fix this but there was nothing.

"S-susan?" She called out.

Nothing, not a single sound.

Beth. Beth. Beth.

She'd thought that Beth's desire for a partner who made her feel safe by making decisions was toxic but she was starting to think that it was the opposite. Beth would always be soft spoken, be kind unless the rights of the people she loved were trampled on – as she'd defended Anna before the Unvaredonia elders and how she continued to defend Carrie despite her shortcomings. Beth would fight everybody's battle but her own.

Anna on the other hand was a lawyer, even though she'd said her job wasn't a matter of passion, in a sense, she was a protector, a fierce defender of her clients. She wasn't like Beth, she was a warrior and she would fight for Beth. While Beth protected those she loved, Anna would in turn protect her; take on the battles she wouldn't fight.

That was exactly what she needed to do; to let Beth know that she would fight for her; by her side. Anna had thought that the both of them were being brave and selfless by sacrificing their happiness and themselves, but it could also be fighting for something that they both deserved. Anna would teach Beth the true meaning of the word.

***

Beth was tired of waiting, she'd checked the back garden but Susan and Anna were nowhere to be found. The rest of the tenants were gathered in the living room with Beth – ever since Beth's outburst ten minutes ago, Nancy had been mostly quiet, looking at Beth in a new light as if she was just seeing her for the first time.

She was thinking of heading outside, walking until she found Anna and told her what her heart was bursting to tell her. And there was something she needed to tell Susan too, but that one could be told to the rest of the tenants and they would tell Susan themselves.

Beth cleared her throat, breaking through the conversation that the three of them were happening. "If I could please have your attention." She felt like the best friend at a wedding giving the toast, she felt giddy too.

All three pairs of eyes turned to her.

"I know that you've already figured this out but the real reason that Anna and I came here was because I was planning to move here, I was going to find a way to settle with you so that I could move in with my girlfriend – Anyways, I have no intentions to send you people out of this house. It's your home and I can't take that away from you." Beth said and meaning it too.

"We weren't going to let you anyways." Nancy called out but she was smiling.

"Oh, there they are." Felicity said, facing the stairway where Susan and Anna were descending.

"You made your decision." Anna said, announcing that she heard what Beth told to the tenants.

Beth spun around, she wasn't sure who moved first but then the two of them were embracing each other. "I'm so sorry, Anna," Beth continued to say over and over again, she might have shed a few tears too.

They finally pulled away from each other, realising that they had an audience. Anna refused to let go of Beth's hands though. Her hands were a little smaller than Beth's, her fingers were bare, compared to Beth's bright green nail polish. Two opposites yet finding pieces of themselves in each other.

"It's late, we should get going." Beth looked at Susan.

Everyone stand up for a farewell by walking them to the door.

Anna was telling Susan that they would be needing to exchange a new agreement sometime this week when Beth's phone rang. The shrill sound cutting through the lull of conversation, Beth took one look at the screen and frowned.

"It's Carrie." Beth announced.

Anna smirked. "Are you going to tell her we are leaving?"

"I'll text her to meet me in London", Beth said it surely.

She typed:

We need to talk, meet me in my apartment in London.

"So, Anna and I have come to a settlement." Susan said as she walked them down the street to where Anna had parked her car.

Beth cast her a side glance. "What? There's nothing to negotiate. The house is rightfully yours, Susan, I'm grateful for how you've maintained the property.”

“The house is a part of you, Beth, a gift from your aunt. Anna and I have come to a decision; you and Anna can move in with us, or take a trip here whenever and however suits you. Before you say anything, there are four bedrooms. Simon and Felicity share one and Hunter and Nancy share the other. That leaves a room for you and Anna. You already feel like family.”

Tears welled up in Beth’s eyes, blurring her vision. She was thinking of her aunt, who’d unwittingly led Beth to the greatest happiness of her life. She turned to Anna.

“I don’t know what to say,” Beth murmured.

“Say you’ll be back.”

***

There was a song playing on the radio, Beth didn’t know it but she hummed the melody. Anna was squarely facing the road ahead as she drove, but her free hand was resting on Beth’s thigh. This, Beth realised; this was what it felt like to belong.

www.ingramcontent.com/pod-product-compliance
Lightning Source LLC
Chambersburg PA
CBHW021127070726
47591CB00014B/1682

9 781915 557179